The cruel death of Robin of Sherwood at the hands of the wicked Sheriff of Nottingham knocked all the fight out of the little band of outlaws. Soon Sherwood Forest and the surrounding villages were again left at the mercy of the unscrupulous men who held their power from King John. The days of Robin Hood seemed destined to pass into the realms of legends. And yet there were some who refused to believe he was dead and rumours flew that Robin of Sherwood, Herne's son, was still alive. Even the outlaws themselves could not be sure – they saw Robin fall, cut down by a hail of arrows – but who was the mysterious hooded man who rescued the rest of them from the onslaught?

Only one man knows – Robert of Huntingdon. For it was he who was summoned by Herne to become the hooded man at that time of crisis for the outlaws. But Robert is a rich young nobleman, with no desire to give up his comfortable existence to live the raw and dangerous life of an outlaw – until an encounter with the barbarous Owen of Clun (one of King John's more dubious allies) leaves Robert with no choice but to run for his life.

His first task is to find and reunite the scattered outlaws of Sherwood, prove himself to them and resume the mantle of the hooded man. Spurred on by the desire to avenge himself on Owen of Clun, Robert's task is given a new urgency when he hears that Marion of Leaford is in Owen's power and in terrible danger!

Richard Carpenter's *Robin of Sherwood* series on television has become popular and this new book is based upon the first three episodes of the new series. *Robin of Sherwood* and *Robin of Sherwood and the Hounds of Lucifer* are also available in Puffin.

Other books by Richard Carpenter

RICHARD CARPENTER'S

ROBIN OF SHERWOOD: THE HOODED MAN

---

by Anthony Horowitz

PUFFIN BOOKS

Puffin Books, Penguin Books Ltd, Harmondsworth, Middlesex, England
Viking Penguin Inc., 40 West 23rd Street, New York, New York 10010, U.S.A.
Penguin Books Australia Ltd, Ringwood, Victoria, Australia
Penguin Books Canada Limited, 2801 John Street, Markham, Ontario, Canada L3R 1B4
Penguin Books (N.Z.) Ltd, 182–190 Wairau Road, Auckland 10, New Zealand

First published 1986

Made and printed in Great Britain by
Richard Clay (The Chaucer Press) Ltd,
Bungay, Suffolk
Filmset in 10/11½ Monophoto Baskerville by
Northumberland Press Ltd, Gateshead,
Tyne and Wear

CONTENTS

PROLOGUE

'Robin Hood is dead.'

The rain swept down across Sherwood Forest, dripping through the trees and pattering on to the ground. The sky was an unbroken grey, the clouds pressed together in hopeless confusion. That summer it seemed the rain had never stopped, washing the colour out of the land and exhausting man and animal alike. Nothing moved in the forest. All was silent but for the drip, drip, drip of the water spitting down into ever-widening pools.

'Robin Hood is dead.'

The Sheriff of Nottingham whispered the words to himself as he lay in his bed, listening to the rain. A fire had been built on the stone floor beside his bed, but it had long gone out and he shivered in the morning cold. For the hundredth time he thought back to the events of a year before, to the death of the one man he had most hated – most feared.

King John had ordered him to hunt down Robin Hood or to lose his own head. And he had hunted him down, like an animal. One after another the outlaws had been captured until only their leader was left. And then at last Robin Hood had fallen, cut down by a hail of arrows, and his body had been buried deep in the heart of the forest. There would be no memorial to Robin Hood, no martyr's grave. He would be forgotten.

'Robin Hood is dead.'

The Sheriff had drunk deep of the cup of victory that day, but by evening the taste had become sour. It was still difficult to understand what had happened. The outlaws – Little John, Will Scarlet, the Saracen Nasir and Friar Tuck, the renegade monk – had been his prisoners. He had had them in his power but then, somehow, he had lost them.

Who was the hooded man? He had come out of the forest, cut his way into the hut where the outlaws were imprisoned and released them. For a moment he had stood in front of the Sheriff and defied him. And the Sheriff's soldiers had been afraid to move. That was the incredible thing. They were fools, simpletons – but it was almost as if they believed that the ghost of Robin Hood had returned to haunt them.

'He's dead. He has to be.'

The Sheriff turned over in his bed and gazed at the tapestry on the wall – a bright summer scene designed to give some illusion of warmth. It had been a good year. The outlaws seemed to have vanished from Sherwood Forest. Only Marion, the so-called wife of Robin Hood (the so-called widow, the Sheriff muttered to himself) was still present in Nottingham. Somehow her father, Sir Richard of Leaford, had managed to beg or buy a pardon from the king. But she was nothing to him. Alone she was powerless.

And without Robin Hood, the Sheriff had had a free hand in the shire. Taxes that year had been high, but nobody had stopped him from collecting them. The roads through Sherwood Forest were safe at last. And there was nobody to protest when some wretched peasant had to be whipped or some poacher lost his right hand to the sword.

It had been a good year. Robin Hood was dead. So why couldn't the Sheriff sleep?

The people thought that he was still alive. They wouldn't believe that they had heard the last of Robin Hood ... and somehow, deep inside him, the Sheriff didn't believe it either. A hooded man had come out of the forest to rescue the outlaws. Not Robin Hood, but ... who?

The Sheriff pulled the rough linen sheets over his head, closed his eyes and tried once again to sleep.

1. A BANQUET

The man on the grey horse was richly dressed in a light blue riding-cloak fastened at the neck with a buckle of pure gold. Now, with the sun at last shining in a cloudless sky, he galloped through the forest on a task which in all honesty he wished he had not been given. But when your father is the Earl of Huntingdon, one of the most powerful men in the country, and when such a father tells you to do something, it is generally wiser to obey.

The reason for his journey was meanwhile riding in the opposite direction towards him. The Sheriff of Nottingham – along with another hundred guests – had been invited to Huntingdon Castle. His steward, Guy of Gisburne, rode with him, and his brother, the Abbot Hugo (who had never even learnt to ride) trundled along beside them on a cart. There was to be a banquet and the Sheriff had been invited, not because the Earl had any particular liking for him, but because his official presence would add weight to the proceedings.

'We wouldn't have been doing this a year ago, would we, Gisburne?' the Sheriff was saying as he sniffed the cold morning air.

'My lord?' Gisburne asked.

'Riding through Sherwood.'

'There are still outlaws in Sherwood,' Gisburne reminded his master.

'But no Robin Hood,' the Sheriff said. 'No leader.'

'Try convincing the people,' Hugo scowled. As a matter of fact, the Abbot very rarely did anything but scowl. Even when he smiled he still managed to twist his lips into a sort of upwards scowl.

'The Abbot's right,' Gisburne agreed. 'They simply refuse

to believe he's dead. If you'd brought the body to Notting-ham ...'

'It was unrecognizable, Gisburne!' the Sheriff cut in angrily. He had had this argument before, and not just with Gisburne. Hubert de Giscard, the king's personal steward, had himself demanded to see the evidence of Robin Hood's death, but by then it had been too late. 'I wonder what happened to the others?' he mused, changing the subject. 'Will Scarlet, Little John and that filthy Saracen ...'

'I'll track them down,' Gisburne promised, 'however long it takes. And the man who rescued them.'

'Of course you will, Gisburne.' The Sheriff smiled sarcasti-cally. 'I've enormous faith in your abilities.'

'Hah!' Hugo sniffed.

It was then that they saw the man on the grey horse. The Sheriff pulled in his reins and regarded the rider with disdain. He was obviously the son of some nobleman. You could tell as much just by glancing at the horse. It was a destrier, a knight's horse, probably brought into England from Ireland. It would have cost at least sixty pounds in Nottingham market ... a small fortune. The boy was well dressed too. Even his riding-cloak was a light blue in colour, rather than the heavier – and cheaper – woad which most riders wore.

'My lords,' the young man said, bowing his head, 'I've come to escort you to the castle.'

Hugo turned to his brother with a contemptuous sneer. 'And who is this peacock?' he demanded.

The young man seemed more amused than annoyed by the slight. 'I'm Huntingdon,' he said, 'Robert of Huntingdon. The Earl is my father.'

The Sheriff and the Abbot exchanged glances. Robert of Huntingdon turned his horse round and began the slow journey back to the castle. He did not like his father's guests. He had heard many stories of the Sheriff's cruelty and the Abbot's greed. But such things did not concern him. They were nothing to do with him ... were they?

Yet he still remembered the madness that had come on him

almost exactly a year ago. A voice had called him out of Huntingdon Castle, a voice that seemed to come from inside his head. It had been like a dream. There had been a lake and a man with the horns and head of a stag. The man had called himself Herne ... Herne the Hunter, spirit of the forest. And he had addressed Robert as his son.

Guided by Herne – or perhaps enchanted by him – Robert had rescued the outlaws who had once followed the man called Robin Hood. A hood had hidden his own features. Now, as he rode back to the castle, he couldn't help smiling to himself. He wondered what the Sheriff would say if he knew that it had been he – Robert of Huntingdon – who had defied him and for a moment had his arrow aimed at the Sheriff's throat.

'You were chosen,' Herne had said. And, 'You will return.'

A year had passed and Robert had not returned. He was the only son and heir of the richest Earl in the country. One day a great castle and a fortune would be his. How could he give all that up for the life of an outlaw in Sherwood Forest? It was out of the question.

Behind him, the Sheriff laughed loudly at one of his own jokes. Robert of Huntingdon shuddered with disgust, gritted his teeth and rode on.

Huntingdon Castle was indeed a great castle, one of the finest in the country. It was as far removed from the old motte-and-bailey constructions that had been found at the time of the Conquest and which still littered the countryside as a destrier is from a donkey. It was a true concentric castle, inspired by the great fortresses that the crusaders had seen in the East. Its walls were fifteen feet thick, topped with battlements and machicolations – gaps through which huge boulders might be rolled or boiling liquid poured. The castle was impregnable, except perhaps against the privations of a long siege. Break in through the gatehouse and you would still have to fight your way across the barbican. Reach the other side of the barbican and a narrow passage would stand between you and the main courtyard. It would seem to an attacker that

-11-

behind every wall lay another, higher wall. But Huntingdon Castle had never been attacked. It was more than a home to the Earl of Huntingdon: it was a living symbol of his power.

The Sheriff of Nottingham was not the only important guest invited to the castle that day. Even as he rode towards it, a tall, elderly man was moving through the great hall to kneel before the Earl. His name was Sir Richard of Leaford. But it was not Sir Richard himself who drew the excited murmurs from the crowd. It was the young girl who walked with him. For this was Marion of Leaford, his daughter. Once she had been the wife of Robin Hood.

She walked with her head held high, her eyes set straight ahead. Her face was drawn and pale and she refused to see the courtiers who turned their backs on her or to hear the cruel whispers that followed in her wake.

'She should have been hanged,' the whispers went.

'Then why wasn't she?'

'The king pardoned her.'

'And was she . . . grateful?'

'Why else did he pardon her?'

The Earl of Huntingdon was not altogether delighted to welcome Marion to his castle. He was a rather grim man, a figure of authority who knew just how much his authority was worth. He would have called himself a friend of the king, but in truth he had no friends. His power had set him on a self-made pinnacle and now he stood there alone. But he had known Sir Richard for many years.

He was waiting for his guests as they walked in, a forbidding figure with steel-grey hair, dressed in a black robe ornamented with gold. A hunting hawk – a handsome peregrine – perched on his hand, its head hooded. The Earl took the hawk virtually everywhere, a sign of his own nobility. He would even have taken the hawk into church with him had not the clerks forbidden it.

'You're like your mother,' he said, seeing Marion. 'Only perhaps a little more headstrong.'

The remark brought titters of malicious laughter from the

crowd in the great hall. They knew Marion's history. It was almost incredible that she was now allowed to dine with the Earl.

'Still,' the Earl went on, 'we mustn't dwell on the past, must we? Some things are better forgotten.'

'Some things, my lord.' Marion's voice was almost a whisper and suddenly her eyes were bright with tears.

They were interrupted by the arrival of the Sheriff and his brother, the Abbot, who was complaining loudly about his sore back. If the Earl of Huntingdon had been cold with Marion, with the Sheriff he was positively glacial. He too had heard stories about Robert de Rainault, and (perhaps the only thing he had in common with his son) he hadn't liked what he'd heard.

'Welcome, my lords,' Huntingdon growled. 'I think you know Sir Richard of Leaford and his daughter Marion.'

'We do, my lord,' the Sheriff sneered. 'Although of course, the last time we met she was . . .' He coughed as if the word offended him. '. . . an outlaw.'

'Lady Wolfshead,' Gisburne added with an unpleasant smile.

The atmosphere in the great hall was suddenly as sharp as a dagger's blade. All eyes were on the little group in the centre and even the servants had stopped what they were doing to see what would happen. Sir Richard blushed. He had managed to save his daughter from execution only by going on his knees to King John and – a proud man – it had cost him dear. Marion's behaviour, her time in the forest, horrified him. Often the two had argued. But even an outlaw was preferable to the three smiling creatures who now confronted him – the Sheriff with his bulging eyes and oily manner, his ghoulish, black-capped brother and his ambitious steward.

'The king pardoned her,' he said, trying to control his anger. 'He showed great mercy.'

'Great mercy?' Hugo snapped. 'Astonishing mercy . . . to a traitor!'

'That's enough,' the Earl of Huntingdon said.

'It made me sick!' Hugo went on, ignoring him. 'This woman was an outlaw, married to the most notorious wolfshead in Nottingham, and now we're expected to share a table with her! I . . .'

'Be silent!' Huntingdon shouted. 'I will not have my guests abused.'

Hugo opened his mouth to speak again but this time it was the Sheriff who stopped him. There was nothing to be gained by brawling in the middle of the great hall, surrounded by servants. Already this ugly scene had marred the banquet to come and there were more pressing matters at hand. He reached out and grabbed hold of his brother's arm. For a moment nobody spoke. Then, as if on cue, the minstrels struck up on the lute and drum, the servants hurried forward and the guests began to take their places at the tables.

Robert of Huntingdon had watched all this with mixed feelings. Like everybody else, he had heard a great deal about Marion and had looked forward to meeting her. Now that he had seen her with his own eyes, he found himself strangely moved. She was far more beautiful than he had imagined, with her chestnut hair tumbling down to her shoulders, her slender arms and her pale skin. She was also more fragile. He could feel her sadness as keenly as if it were his own. As he moved to take his place at the table, he managed to catch her eye and bowed to her, but it was as if she hadn't seen him at all. Robert smiled to himself, determined to speak to her the moment an opportunity arose.

The main door of the great hall opened and a herald stepped in.

'The most noble Lord Owen of Clun,' he announced.

Once again, everything stopped. The guest of honour had arrived.

He was a huge, powerfully built man with long black hair, a black beard and black eyes that were tunnels into a soul of the same colour. The guest of honour had been drinking before he arrived, as had the warriors he brought with him, and together they were more like a pack of animals than a supposedly noble household. They snarled and roared their laughter. They tore at their food with hands like claws. They drank more – and the more they drank the wilder they became.

'The most noble Lord Owen of Clun' was not the sort of man you would normally have expected to find gracing the table of the Earl of Huntingdon. He wasn't the sort of man that the Earl would have trusted even to work in his stables. But he was the reason for this banquet and no matter how drunk or how outrageous his behaviour, he was to be honoured – given pride of place at the high table – and his every whim was to be obeyed.

The year was 1209 and King John was secretly planning to lead an army against the Welsh king, Llewellyn the Great, to make him bow to the English throne.

Wales had been nothing but trouble, ever since the very earliest days of the Conquest. The south had fallen easily enough, but the north – with its hills and mountains – had proved more difficult. If the northern Welshmen had managed to unite themselves, instead of living apart in warring tribes, they might have proved a real threat to the English throne. Such a threat had at last arrived in the person of Llewellyn, the most popular king the Welsh had yet had. Although he had acknowledged himself the vassal of King John, he was still tugging at the leash, striving for independence ... and the

Welsh people were slowly uniting behind him. That was why King John was about to take punitive action.

But to make matters more difficult still, there were the Marcher lords to consider. When William the Conqueror had ridden into Wales, he had allowed a number of great lordships to spring up along the border between the two countries. It was a mistake that his successors had often regretted. The Marcher lords, as they were known, had become strong. They owned private armies and ran their own system of justice. They were English to the English and Welsh to the Welsh, but in fact they belonged to neither country. They were their own men, loyal only to themselves.

Owen of Clun was one of them; no Marcher lord was more powerful. And it was on him that the outcome of King John's war with the Welsh would depend.

If King John were to hope for success, he would need Owen on his side. His soldiers would have to pass through Owen's territory to reach the enemy, and that would be impossible without the lord's permission. Moreover, if Owen were actually to join the English with his private army, victory would be assured. That was why the banquet had been arranged. King John needed Owen of Clun.

No expense had been spared for the Marcher lord's pleasure. The great hall of Huntingdon Castle had been filled with every man of note in the area ... sheriffs, abbots, earls and knights. Costly beeswax candles burned in the holders and the nefs on the table – the little boxes that contained a private napkin, a knife and spoons for an honoured guest – were of solid silver. The food was as spectacular as the setting. There were three courses, each course containing the same mixture of sweet and savoury dishes that could be eaten in any order. An ox had been slaughtered for the feast, roasted in the kitchen and sliced up at the carving-table. Only the finest French wine flowed at the high table, although the lower tables had to make do with strong ale. The chef had excelled himself with a subtlety – a castle made of pastry and coated with nuts and marzipan – which was the centrepiece of the banquet. Instead of the usual honey, the bowls on the tables were filled with sugar – an unheard of luxury, for it had been imported at great cost all the way from Spain. And while the guests ate, minstrels played and sang, telling stories of the exploits of King Arthur and his knights of the round table – stories which everyone knew but which they were always pleased to hear again.

And yet it was an uneasy alliance. Two more different men than Huntingdon and Owen would be hard to imagine. Huntingdon spent his days hunting and practising the chivalric skills at the tourney. He kept falcons and fine horses. He attended Mass three times a day and even read the occasional book. Owen of Clun preferred to spend his days watching men die.

Only twenty-four hours before the feast, his champion had killed for him again. Every week there were fights in Owen's castle – fights to the death watched by a throng of drinking, laughing Marcher warriors. He had built a special arena for these blood games, a great wooden circle around a dusty pit where the fighters, armed with two swords each, could fight it out in the manner of the ancient gladiators. The last fight had been spectacular, lasting almost half an hour. The challenger had been fast and bold. But Owen's champion had finally mastered him, plunging his sword into the other man's heart, killing him instantly, and winning his master a small fortune in won bets.

Now Owen smiled as more food and wine were served at the high table. He grabbed his manchet – a hunk of wheaten bread – and spread it thick with butter, using his thumb. Then he dipped it into his gravy, ignoring the glances of the other guests. It was usually considered a sign of good breeding to save the manchet for the poor who flocked to the castle walls – but what did Owen care about good breeding? A servant filled his goblet and he drained it again as quickly. He knew that he was being courted, that his allegiance was needed against the Welsh. And he meant to enjoy himself.

He leant back in his chair and looked about him. That was when he saw Marion.

She was sitting next to the fair-haired youth, the Earl's son or whoever he was. Owen had no interest in him. But the girl . . . There was something about her that excited him. She was beautiful, true. But she was spirited too. He could sense it in her. Owen of Clun had no idea who she was, nor did he care. Suddenly he wanted her. That was all that mattered.

Robert of Huntingdon glanced up and saw Owen of Clun looking in their direction.

'Lord Owen is watching you,' he whispered to Marion. 'I think you should keep away from him.'

Marion looked at Robert more thoughtfully. 'I intend to,' she said.

The minstrels struck up again and the company rose to dance. A young lord led Marion on to the dance-floor and Robert followed close behind, partnering a lady whose name he had already forgotten. He was worried. Although Owen had not stood up to join in the dance, he could see that the Marcher lord's eyes were still fixed on Marion. He knew that something was going to happen.

The dance was a sort of pavane – a slow, formal reel in which the dancers change partners as the music directs. So it was that Marion, following the correct steps, moved across, turned and suddenly found herself standing next to Guy of Gisburne, the blond-haired, grinning steward to the Sheriff of Nottingham.

'Did you dance in Sherwood?' he asked cruelly as he took her hand. Marion pivoted slowly in time with the music. 'Perhaps you don't remember – Lady Wolfshead,' Gisburne added with a thin smile.

Then mercifully the music changed again and this time she found herself partnered by Robert. She had barely spoken to him throughout the banquet, but she was glad to find herself next to him. Robert noticed her distress.

'Gisburne?' he asked quietly.

'I wish he was dead,' Marion muttered.

A few minutes later the music returned Marion to her original partner, then came to an end. The young lords bowed, the women curtsied. There was applause from the banqueters who sat at the long tables and the dancers began to move back towards their chairs. Then Owen struck.

He had watched the dance with a strange, burning hunger. Never once had his eyes left Marion. Once he had whispered, as if to himself, 'By Satan – how she moves!'

The oath had been overheard by one of his warrior knights but by nobody else. And now, suddenly, he was standing on the dance-floor, swaying slightly from the effects of the wine, only a few inches away from Marion.

'Again!' he cried so that everyone in the great hall could hear. 'You will dance again!'

For a moment nobody was quite sure what to do. Almost unconsciously, Robert's hand had gone to the dagger that he wore at his belt. Marion stood helpless, her way blocked by Owen. The young lord who had been her partner grew pale and abandoned her to her fate. The musicians were silent. Only the Sheriff of Nottingham and his brother were unable to keep the smiles from their faces. As far as they were concerned, whatever happened to Marion couldn't be bad enough.

Then the Earl of Huntingdon stood up. Owen of Clun was his guest. He had been given a mission by the king. Nothing else mattered. He signalled to the minstrels and the music began again. This time Owen and Marion were alone on the dance-floor. Robert took his place at his table. He was disgusted by his father's behaviour. One of his guests – the Lady Marion – had been compromised. The Earl should have stopped it.

But the Earl only watched as Owen and Marion danced. Owen was barely moving, ignoring the music. His eyes were locked into hers. He watched as she went through the motions of the dance, her body swaying and turning. The sweat glistened on his forehead. His lips, almost hidden by the black beard and moustache, were wet.

Then he seized her. As the music faltered and stopped, he pulled her towards him. His lips moved towards her cheek.

But Marion had been expecting it. At the last minute she managed to break free, stepped back and swung a hand with all her might. The slap was like a thunder-clap in the crowded hall. Owen's head lashed back, his eyes staring. But he seemed to feel no pain.

For perhaps five seconds he stood in silence. It could have been five hours. Nobody knew what the Marcher lord would do. Would he kill the girl? Would he walk out? Slowly, he lifted a hand and rubbed the cheek where she had hit him. Then he smiled. The smile broadened into a laugh. His whole body shook as the laughter became louder, a laughter that his followers took up and amplified. Soon everyone in the hall was laughing – everyone except Marion's father and Robert. And, of course, Marion. Bright red with anger and humiliation she walked back to her seat.

'I think I'm in love!' Owen sang out after her.

More laughter. Now his men were cheering and applauding too. With tears of joy running from his eyes, Owen turned to go back to his place ... and found himself facing Robert of Huntingdon. The smile faded from Owen's lips. At the same time, the laughter became uncertain, then died away. It was incredible. The boy – he was barely more than a boy – was obstructing him. His hand was on his sword.

'Will you apologize, my lord?' Robert demanded.

'Apologize?' Owen repeated the word in a whisper. 'What did you say?'

'Robert!' The Earl of Huntingdon had got to his feet and was trying to stop him.

Robert ignored his father. 'You heard me,' he said to Owen.

Pure anger sobered Owen of Clun as quickly as a pail of icy water. 'You insolent puppy!' he snarled, drawing his sword. 'I'll cut you into pieces!'

'How many pieces?' Robert replied, drawing his own sword.

The fight had begun before anybody realized what was happening. What had a moment ago been a dance-floor had become a deadly arena; the banquet had become a battle. As the swords clashed, the Marcher warriors roared their approval, while the Earl of Huntingdon shouted in vain for his guards to break up the fight, his words lost in the general din.

Owen of Clun was the stronger of the two. He swung his sword like an axe and one blow would have cut Robert in half. But Robert of Huntingdon had been taught the art of swordsmanship as part of his early education and it was indeed a case of art against brute force. Although Owen rained down blows on him, none seemed to come close, while Robert's own thrusts and parries were driving the Marcher lord back. To everyone watching, it was clear that the boy was more than the equal of the man.

Their blades locked and suddenly their hands were touching as the hilts of their swords pressed against each other. A blazing torch jutted out of the wall, and as the two men struggled, their hands came closer and closer to the flames. It had begun as a fight of skill. When the blades had locked it had become a fight of strength. Now, as the flames licked upwards, burning their skin, it became a fight of endurance. Closer and closer their hands moved towards the flames. The swords were almost forgotten.

Then Owen of Clun, unable to bear any more, let out a great yell. He stepped back and dropped his weapon. Shuddering with pain and humiliation, he rubbed his blistered hands together while the crowd watched in silence. It was impossible. But the boy had taken on the lord in front of them all, and the boy had won.

The Earl of Huntingdon, however, took no pride in his son's victory. 'Robert!' he demanded, stepping between the two fighters. 'Have you taken leave of your senses?'

'I want him whipped!' Owen cried. He was stone-cold sober now and more like a spoilt child than a great Marcher nobleman. 'Is this the way you treat your guests, Huntingdon?' he whined. 'I am Owen of Clun!'

The Earl tried to find words to express himself, but there were none. He turned instead to his son who stood there waiting, his sword sheathed, his face emotionless. 'On your knees!' he demanded.

Robert stood where he was.

'Robert!' the Earl shouted. 'I command you!'

Robert said nothing. He dared not speak. He could hardly believe what was happening. Owen of Clun had behaved like a beast. He, Robert, had cut him down to size. His father should have congratulated him. To Robert it seemed that the Earl's behaviour was as cowardly as it was unjust.

He bowed to Marion. Then, ignoring his father, he strode out of the great hall.

Owen watched him go, his black eyes on fire.

'Challenged!' he exclaimed. 'Insulted! Made to look a fool! I came here in friendship . . .'

The Earl of Huntingdon raised his hands to pacify his guest. 'He shall beg forgiveness,' he said. 'I swear it, my lord.'

'Then see it done!' Owen cried. 'See it done, Huntingdon. Or by Thor's hammer no soldier of the king shall cross my lands.'

The Earl of Huntingdon bowed his head. Marion sat in silence, still unsure of what she had just seen. Robert of Huntingdon . . . ? Why had he taken her side? What did she mean to him? And opposite her, the Sheriff of Nottingham drained his goblet, deep in thought. He had watched the fight with amusement and he was only sorry that neither of the fighters – the brute or the brat – had managed to get themselves seriously hurt. So Owen was in love with Marion was he? And Robert had defended her?

Already the Sheriff was wondering how he could use the situation to his own ends. He had wanted Marion dead a year before. But perhaps death would have been too good for her, too easy. He smiled. Yes, perhaps there was another way . . .

3. THE ABDUCTION

Sir Richard of Leaford and Marion left Huntingdon Castle the following morning at first light. Neither father nor daughter had discussed the events of the night before, but both were anxious to put as much space as possible between themselves and Owen of Clun.

'An early start, my lord,' Sir Richard said to his host as he climbed on to his horse outside the main gate. 'I thought it best.'

The Earl of Huntingdon nodded gravely. 'You always were a tactful man, Richard,' he said.

'Thank you, my lord.'

There was an uneasy silence. Sir Richard's manner was courteous and yet something hung in the air ... a sense of accusation. The Earl of Huntingdon felt it and coughed.

'Last night,' he muttered, 'there was nothing I could do. You do ... I mean, I'm sure you understand that.'

'Of course, my lord.'

But both men knew that this was far from the truth. The Earl of Huntingdon could have stopped Owen. He could have prevented that fateful dance with Marion. But he had chosen not to. He had put politics before politeness. In his fear of offending the Marcher lord he had been less than a gentleman, less than a knight.

There was nothing more to be said. Father and daughter as one bade their farewells, turned their horses away from the castle and set off down the dusty track that would eventually lead them back to Leaford Grange. The Earl of Huntingdon watched them go, his mind pondering what had happened at the banquet. He couldn't blame himself; he wouldn't blame himself. He was just glad to see the back of them.

He turned and found himself facing Robert. His son must have been standing behind him all the time. His eyes were far away, following the two riders as they cantered into the distance. For a long while neither man spoke. Then the Earl levelled his grey eyes on Robert.

'You will find Owen,' he commanded. 'You will find him now. And you will apologize for last night's little performance.'

'Apologize?' Robert repeated.

'I was commanded by the king to win him over,' the Earl said. 'What possessed you to . . . ?'

'He insulted her.'

'Insulted her?' The Earl's anger exploded at last. 'Marion of Leaford is beyond insult. That woman is notorious! Insult her? You should worry more about what you've done to me. Where's your respect? Your sense of duty? You are my son, the heir to an earldom – but look at you! An empty-headed fool who thinks of nothing but falcons and horses!'

A gust of wind blew in from the forest and Robert shivered. It was as if an invisible knife had severed something between his father and him. For many years – ever since his mother had died – the two men had grown apart, each following a path that led in a different direction. Now, at last, they had reached a point where they could no longer see each other.

'Find Lord Owen and humble yourself before him,' the Earl commanded. 'Do it now, boy!'

Robert turned and strode into the castle, his father following close behind. Without looking back or faltering in his pace, he marched into the great hall, the scene of last night's banquet. But any sense of festivity had flickered out with the last flames of the braziers. Owen of Clun was asleep in a chair, tilted back away from the table, his mouth wide open, snoring. His men lay sprawled around him, some spread-eagled on the floor, others propped up against the furniture. The air was heavy with the smell of sweat and stale wine.

As his father reached the entrance, Robert approached

Owen of Clun. His hand stretched out as if to wake the man – but instead it caught hold of the back of the chair, pushing it beyond the point of balance. The next moment, the Marcher lord had toppled over backwards, hitting the floor with an ear-splitting crash. His eyes flashed open. His men awoke, some of them fumbling groggily for their swords. Shaking his head, Owen staggered to his feet. The first person he saw was the Earl of Huntingdon.

'Who did it?' he snarled. 'Who did it?' He spun round, but Robert had already gone. 'It was your idiot son, wasn't it?' he continued, grimacing furiously at the Earl. 'Wasn't it?'

'My lord . . .' the Earl began. He still didn't believe what he had just seen.

'This place is a madhouse!' Owen cried. 'I'm not staying a moment longer.'

'I beg you, my lord . . .' It was a nightmare. It had to be. It couldn't really be happening.

'The king will hear of this,' Owen promised. 'The king will hear how I've been baited and bullied and belittled. By Odin's beard, I wouldn't stay in this accursed pile of dung for half the royal exchequer!'

'The Lord of Clun has spoken!' a warrior gurgled feebly.

'I have spoken!' Owen agreed. 'And I'll speak this too. If that boy ever comes near me again, I'll tear him to shreds. I'll tear him into a hundred pieces. And I'll do it with my bare hands!'

With that, the Marcher lord marched out of the room with his warriors, leaving the Earl wishing that he had never heard of Owen of Clun, Marion of Leaford – or, for that matter, Robert of Huntingdon.

The whole scene had been witnessed by a man standing silently on a balcony above. The Sheriff of Nottingham was very skilled at not being noticed when it suited him. He was a man of shadows; shadows were his natural habitat. Now he slunk forward, hurried down a staircase and followed Owen out to the stables. He reached him just as he was about to mount his horse.

'My lord,' he hissed.

'Yes?' Owen of Clun glanced down at the graceless creature who had addressed him. Slowly he recalled who this creature was. 'What do you want, Sheriff?' he demanded.

The Sheriff looked left and right. There was nobody about apart from Owen's men. 'The girl,' he said, 'Marion . . .'

Owen's eyes narrowed. Inside him, the flame that had been kindled the night before sparked again. 'What of her?' he asked.

'I just thought you might like to know that she'll have taken the Leaford road.'

'To Leaford?'

'Her home.'

Owen smiled. It was a diabolical smile. A wolf's smile. 'To horse!' he shouted. 'To horse!'

The Sheriff stood still as Owen's men mounted their horses all around him. He stood still as they whipped them and stormed out, the hoofs clattering on the cobbled stones. Only when they had vanished in a cloud of dust and loose straw did he walk back into the castle. He was pleased with himself. He had sown his seeds of poison. He wondered what sort of harvest they would bring.

Huntingdon Castle was about an hour's ride behind them. Sir Richard and Marion were riding slowly, at no more than a trot, glad simply to be on their way home. Their path had led them through a stretch of woodland, but now it sloped gently down to run parallel with a stream. It was a hot day. The flies were buzzing around the sweat on the horses' flanks and bothering the riders.

'Let's rest,' Sir Richard said.

Marion smiled gratefully. Her father dismounted and helped her down from her saddle. Then they led the horses to the stream, sat down themselves and drank from their water-bottles. A kingfisher swooped down out of the sunlight. There was a brief eruption on the surface of the stream, then it flew off again, a tiny fish struggling in its beak.

Marion had seen this and suddenly she shivered.

'Father . . .' she muttered.

'What is it?' Sir Richard's eyes were heavy.

'Father, there's . . .' But how could she tell him? Her years in the forest with Robin Hood had tuned her senses to danger. The snapping of a twig, a light in the darkness, a patch of trampled grass where the grass should have grown straight . . . any of them could mean sudden peril. Over the years she had developed an instinct, a sort of inner warning-system. And she could feel it now, prickling under her skin.

'Father,' she said, 'we must go. Now.'

'What's the matter?'

But then Sir Richard saw what his daughter had merely felt. There were six riders. They had appeared on the brow of the hill, on the opposite side of the stream. Now they hung there, silhouetted against the sky, the horses snorting and shaking their manes. His head snapped round. Another six men were riding down the track towards them. Owen of Clun was at their head.

'Get to your horse,' Sir Richard whispered, his hand reaching for his sword.

'No . . .' Marion began.

'Do as I say!' he commanded, but his voice was kind.

Marion couldn't argue. A moment later Owen's men charged, coming down on them from both sides. The water boiled as the six horses plunged into the stream. Sir Richard had drawn his sword. As the first of the Marcher warriors reached him, it flashed through the air. There was a yell. Marion reached her horse. Her hand stretched out to take the reins, but then an arm seized her, curling round her throat. She turned round to see Owen of Clun leering as he pulled her towards him.

'If I want something,' he laughed, 'I take it.'

Marion lashed out with both hands, but this time Owen was ready for her. The blows missed and then she was on the ground, bruised and dazed. The world turned a cart-wheel. She saw her father running towards her, saw a sword scythe through the air behind him, heard him give a muffled cry. He fell; his blood stained the grass. Owen seized hold of her.

Then there was nothing.

4. NASIR

Twenty-four hours after Marion had been taken, Sir Richard stood in front of the Sheriff of Nottingham. He was pale from loss of blood; a purple gash on the side of his head showed where the edge of a blade had hit him. Owen's men had left him for dead, but he was alive. And he was determined to win Marion back whatever the cost.

'A little more braid around the collar . . .'

The Sheriff seemed more interested in a new robe that he was ordering from his tailor than in the wounded knight with his tales of kidnap and attempted murder. His brother, the Abbot Hugo, crouched over a sheaf of papers, sniffed noisily. Sir Guy of Gisburne regarded him with cold disdain.

'I need soldiers,' Sir Richard said.

'Why come to us?' The Sheriff waved his tailor away with a limp hand. 'Why not your friend the Earl of Huntingdon?'

'Because his hands are tied by the king.'

'And so are mine.' The Sheriff smiled. 'And for the same reason. King John wants Owen's friendship. If he ever learnt that I'd given you soldiers to fight against him, he'd have my head.'

The Sheriff's attention wandered once again to the rich velvet gowns displayed for him at the bottom of his chamber. Sir Richard sighed. He hadn't wanted to come to the Sheriff — but he had no one else to turn to. The cost of Marion's pardon from the king had been dear. He had no soldiers of his own nor the money to raise them. He couldn't approach the Earl of Huntingdon. There was no one.

'What would you pay me for these soldiers?' the Sheriff asked. He allowed a pause to hang in the air. 'Five hundred marks?'

'Five . . . ?' Sir Richard shook his head. 'That's extortion.'

'Not with the risk involved.'

And now the Sheriff's eyes were on him, daring him to refuse. Given soldiers, he could attack Owen's castle, rescue Marion. If he left her there, anything could happen to her . . . could be happening to her now. He had no choice.

'All right – I'll get it for you,' he said. 'But I need the men at once.'

'And when will I have the money?' the Sheriff demanded.

'At . . . at the end of the month.'

'On what security?'

For the first time the Abbot looked up. 'His lands and Leaford Grange,' he said, curling his lip.

Sir Richard stood, rooted to the spot. It was blackmail. The Sheriff and his brother knew perfectly well that he would never be able to raise such a huge sum in less than twenty days. They were stealing his lands from under his feet. But what else could he do?

'Agreed,' he said.

And at once the Abbot busied himself, his quill-pen scurrying across the paper to produce a legally binding contract. Wax was at hand to take the imprint from Sir Richard's signet-ring. Guy of Gisburne stood by as a witness.

'It's just a safeguard,' the Sheriff explained with a smile. 'Nothing more. And to show my good will, I'll let you have Gisburne for nothing.'

This was news to Gisburne.

'My lord!' he exploded.

'Don't argue, Gisburne,' the Sheriff continued. 'You could do with the exercise. And, by the way, blank shields for the men. I don't want Owen to know where they came from.' He glanced at Sir Richard. 'You can have them tomorrow. The contract will have been drawn up by then.'

Sir Richard looked at the Abbot who was writing with more fervour than he had ever brought to a religious text. He could feel the disgust rising within him, but there was nothing more to be said. One last time his eyes met those of the Sheriff. Then he bowed and left.

'I must protest, my lord,' Gisburne began, as soon as the door had closed.

'You're going, Gisburne,' the Sheriff snapped. 'And so is a messenger to Lord Owen of Clun. Immediately. He must be warned against Sir Richard's foolishness.'

'But . . .' Gisburne frowned. 'If Lord Owen knows we're coming . . . we'll be ambushed . . . massacred!'

'Ambushed – yes,' the Sheriff agreed. 'But not massacred, you idiot. The moment you're attacked you'll run. All of you. Leaving Sir Richard alone.'

At last Gisburne understood and despite himself he marvelled at his master's cunning. Abbot Hugo finished writing and threw down the quill with a malevolent smile.

'The contract,' he said, holding up the sheet of paper.

The Sheriff took it. 'Not a contract,' he muttered. 'A will.'

Gisburne and Sir Richard left Nottingham the following morning at first light, some forty men following behind them. The Sheriff's soldiers carried neither shields nor banners, an anonymous army. It was a long march, but the two men barely spoke to each other. As they drew close to Owen's castle on the Welsh border, it seemed that the colour faded from the land and the grass seemed grey rather than green. The wind moaned softly across the barren plain and the clouds folded over in the sky. There was going to be a storm. The light was a strange, menacing blue and the air was heavy and oppressed.

'Clun Castle is just over the next ridge,' Gisburne said at last.

The words were no sooner out of his mouth than the trap was sprung. The Sheriff's messenger had reached Owen the night before and now there were two dozen men waiting for them, concealed along the ridge. With a great cry they leapt forward, some on horses, some scuttling across the ground on foot.

Sir Richard didn't hesitate. Drawing his sword, he spurred his horse forward, expecting Gisburne and his men to do the same. He had covered perhaps twenty yards when he realized he was alone. Gisburne had fled. His men had scattered. They hadn't even made a pretence of joining in the fight. And then he realized: the Sheriff had betrayed him. He would die alone in a desolate field. His quest had been hopeless before it had even begun.

Sheer anger ran through his blood, lending him strength. His sword raised, he plunged into the mass of Owen's men, slashing left and right. If he was to die, as all men must, then at least he would take a few of them with him.

The ambush had been watched by a figure sitting on a horse, hidden by a clump of trees some distance away. From such a distance an ordinary man would have been unable to see, let alone recognize, Gisburne's face, but this man did and it brought a shimmer of hatred to his eyes. The man was not English. His skin was too dark, his hair and curling beard too black. The single oath he whispered to himself was in a language that no one in England would have understood.

The man's name was Nasir. He was a Saracen and once he had ridden with Robin Hood.

It was chance that had brought him to this part of the country, but it was a cold fury that now propelled him forward. He knew Gisburne. And he knew Sir Richard, Marion's father. What the two men should be doing together here, so close to Wales, he did not know. But this was clearly no time to ask for explanations.

Sir Richard had killed three of his opponents before Nasir reached him. As the unknown horseman swooped down on them from behind, Owen's men scattered and regrouped. But not all of them. Nasir's sword flashed twice. Two men fell to the ground and lay still.

'Nasir!' Sir Richard was breathing heavily. His sword-arm had been wounded and his shirt was drenched in blood. Now he looked at Nasir as if he had sprung out of a dream.

'Ride!' Nasir said.

Gisburne and his soldiers had long since disappeared and there were still nineteen of Owen's men alive. Hopeless odds.

As the two men turned their horses, the Marcher warriors thundered across the field towards them.

'That way!'

Nasir wheeled to the left and pointed to the right. It was an old battle trick. They separated, dividing the strength of the enemy behind them as ten went one way and nine the other. At least one of them might now get away.

But Nasir's luck had run out. He had lost his sword in the first struggle and galloping into a narrow gulley he found his way blocked by reinforcements. Another six men had appeared out of nowhere. He spun round, but his pursuers were close behind. Some had ridden across the top of the gulley. They were on all sides, above and below him. They closed in.

Nasir leapt from his horse, hurling himself at a Marcher warrior who rode close by. The two men tumbled to the ground. Even as he fell, Nasir reached for a dagger, concealed in a sheath at his ankle. The dagger darted like a snake's tongue, and when he stood up he was holding a dead man's sword.

Surrounded by a small army, half of them on horseback, and armed only with a sword, an ordinary man would have surrendered. But Nasir had once been a member of the Saracen sect of Assasseens – professional killers. He was no more able to surrender than he was to fly. Again and again his sword found its mark, but at last a blow caught him on the head. He fell back. A second later, ten swords were slanting down towards his throat.

Meanwhile, Sir Richard had escaped. Weak and bloodied, he guided his horse away from the field. Once he was sure that there was nobody following him, he stopped and turned round, waiting for Nasir. But Nasir didn't come. The sun was setting and Sir Richard shivered in the evening chill. Everything was silent. Still there was no sign of the Saracen.

At last he pulled at the reins and began the slow journey back to Leaford Grange. He rode with a heavy heart. Nasir had been captured. Marion was lost. The Sheriff had betrayed him and unless he found five hundred marks he would forfeit his lands and Leaford Grange too. He had failed when he was most needed.

And there was nobody in the world to whom he could now turn for help.

5. HERNE THE HUNTER

Robert of Huntingdon urged his horse forward, pressing ever deeper into the wilds of Sherwood Forest. He was lost, he knew it, but at the same time he knew exactly where he was going. It made no sense – but then nothing in his life seemed to make much sense any more.

The horse faltered and stopped, its hoofs kicking at the carpet of dead leaves. Robert dug in with his spurs, but the animal was afraid, sensing something that he could not see. Robert swung himself down to the ground, then looped the reins over the branch of a tree. There was a bright glade a little way ahead of him and he walked forward. Suddenly everything was quiet. Even the birds in the trees had ended their songs. It was as if he had crossed some sort of magical barrier and found his way into a different world.

'Why have you come?'

The words were not spoken and yet he heard them. A moment later Herne appeared, the man . . . the spirit . . . the god that he had been searching for. For what was Herne? 'My father,' Robert thought to himself, remembering how Herne had once addressed him as his son. Herne was standing on the brow of a small hill, his body dressed in a cloak of gossamer rags, his head crowned by a pair of sprouting antlers. His face was invisible against the brilliance of the morning light. A white mist rolled around his feet. He seemed to be floating on it.

'I need your help,' Robert said.

'Why should I give it?'

'Because I'm your son.'

'Are you?' The words, still unspoken, were hard. 'You told

me that my son was dead. You denied your destiny and deserted those who would have followed you.'

Robert hung his head. He could not deny all that Herne said. But at that time, a year ago, everything had been different. How could he have known how things would turn out?

'Marion is in danger,' Herne said, as if reading his thoughts.

'What can I do?' Robert pleaded.

Herne gestured and there, lying on the ground beside a great oak tree, was a bow and a quiver of arrows. Robert recognized them at once. He had carried them once before. But then he had been the hooded man.

'Find them,' Herne commanded. 'Little John, Will Scarlet, Nasir and the others. Bring them together. Lead them.'

'Where will I find them?'

'The powers of light and darkness will lead you.' Herne lifted his hands and the mist swirled around him. 'In the past lies what is to come.'

Then the sun found a chink in the leaves of the trees and exploded through the glade. For a moment Herne was swallowed up, obliterated by a shaft of blinding light.

'Bring hope to those who have none, freedom to those in chains, justice to those who have been wronged.'

The words came from the sky, from the earth, from the heart of the light itself. The mist rose and fell. Then a cloud passed across the face of the sun and suddenly Robert found himself alone in the mysterious glade. Behind him, his horse snorted. The birds sang again.

Slowly, he moved forward and picked up the bow.

Meanwhile, Marion was being introduced to her first blood game. Eyes wide with horror, she gazed on the barbaric sport of the Marcher lord. There was the sunken pit, the blazing torches, the crowds of shouting warriors with their wild faces and straggling hair. There was the money passing from hand to hand as bets were placed and lips were licked in cruel anticipation. And there, far below, were the two gladiators, their bare arms extending from their metal breastplates, their heads completely concealed by masks. They were like no masks that Marion had ever seen. Long and pointed, with narrow slits for the eyes and a single horn in the form of a knife-blade curving out of the forehead, they turned the two fighters almost into bird-men. Certainly they were less than human. But nothing about the blood game was remotely human.

'Fine sport!' Owen cried, seizing the back of her neck with a powerful hand. Marion tried to turn away, but he held her fast, forcing her to watch. 'Kill him, you miserable animal!' he screamed as his champion hung back, warding off a blow from his opponent's dagger with his own sword.

'Watch your guard!' This came from the Marcher lord who was seated on the opposite side of the circle. Two hundred marks hung on the outcome of this contest – a small fortune by anyone's standards.

It was all over very quickly. Owen's champion, too confident for his own good, had forced the challenger down to the ground. He stepped over him, his sword raised for the kill, then glanced upwards as if searching for applause. But all he found was a sword in his stomach. His opponent had lashed upwards with the last of his strength. Now blood fountained into the sand at the bottom of the ring. The Marcher warriors roared and laughed. The visiting Marcher lord stood up triumphantly.

'Two hundred marks, Lord Owen!' he sang out.

Owen of Clun was furious. He did not know what angered him more: the loss of his two hundred marks, the loss of his champion or the cowardice of the woman he had brought to be his bride. He looked at Marion now ... hiding her face, tears pouring from her eyes. And why? Because she didn't like the sight of blood? Didn't she enjoy watching brave men die?

Standing up, he gave a signal. At once Marion was led away by two old women attendants who were also her gaolers. Then, forcing a smile to his lips, he paid the Marcher lord his money and stormed out of the arena.

He was followed by a strange and strangely repulsive man who seldom if ever left his side. He was more like a vulture than a man and more like a frog than a vulture. Quite bald, he had pale eyes, a hooked neck and an insane, thin-lipped smile. His name was Gulnar. He was Owen's astrologer and sorcerer.

As soon as the two men were alone, Owen turned to him. 'Is she fit to bear my sons?' he demanded.

'Marion of Leaford?' Gulnar did not speak, he sang, the words quivering in the back of his throat. 'She is, my lord.'

'But where's her spirit?' Owen poured himself a goblet of wine. 'Even the blood game doesn't excite her. What kind of woman is she?'

Gulnar grinned as if the whole thing were some sort of marvellous joke. 'The fire is there,' he simpered. 'It must be kindled.'

'When, Gulnar?'

Gulnar craned his neck forward, the sinews and veins bulging. Slowly, his eyes swivelled round in their sockets until the pupils were almost looking back into his own brain. 'When will she be handfast to the Lord of Clun?' he warbled. 'At the feast of the next moon. On the feast of Arrianrhod. Then and only then.'

Owen's anger welled up again. There were eight days to the next full moon. But he knew better than to argue with Gulnar. The man might be repulsive and insane, but he had never once been wrong. He would just have to wait.

He was still angry as he made his way through the castle and down past the dungeons. Eight whole days until his wedding-night! At least that would give him time to find and train a new champion to replace the fool who had got himself killed. For he would celebrate the wedding with another blood game – and this would be one in which the house of Clun would triumph . . . an omen of a marriage blessed with strong and healthy sons.

A new champion . . .

He had just reached the dungeons when he remembered

the man they had brought in a few days before – the Saracen who had rescued Sir Richard of Leaford. 'A savage wolf' – that was how his captain had described the man. 'A killer, swift and deadly.'

Now Owen walked slowly towards the dungeon, a thought stirring in his mind. Two guards sprang to attention, then – at a signal from their lord – opened the door to allow him to enter. The Saracen was standing against the bare stone wall. He regarded Owen with cold eyes that showed no fear. Eyes that had perhaps never shown fear.

'What do they call you?' Owen demanded.

'Nasir.'

The two syllables were spoken softly, but Owen wondered how many men had trembled to hear them. There was something remarkable about this man. 'You serve Leaford?' he asked.

'I serve no man.'

Owen smiled. 'Then how many men have you killed?'

The Saracen remained silent, but his eyes answered the question. Those cold eyes had seen death ... many deaths. This wasn't just a man. It was a killing machine.

Owen laughed quietly to himself. He had found his new champion.

Edward of Wickham was working on his vegetable garden when the man on the white horse rode into the village. Wiping the sweat from his forehead, he squinted into the sun as the figure moved down towards the stream that ran through the village, a water supply that washed clothes, turned the wheel of the mill and also fed the crops. Now he threw down the hoe he had been working with and straightened up. The figure had drawn close – a young nobleman, fair-haired and richly dressed. Edward walked forward. There wasn't even the hint of a welcoming smile on his face.

Edward was a gentle man by nature, but anger burned deep inside him. Wickham was nothing more than a scattering of cottages and houses with a central barn, a mill and a smithy. Some of the cottages had partially collapsed. The sturdier houses with their whitewashed clay walls and thatched roofs were smoky and damp after the recent rains. There was mud everywhere. It was not a place he would have chosen to live in and yet he had lived there all his life. Edward of Wickham. That was what he had become. For he was as tied to the village as a bullock is tied to a plough and he had just about as much control over his own destiny.

He was a serf. They all were. And what was a serf? Edward had no learning. He couldn't even read. But once he had asked Friar Tuck what it meant.

'It's from the Latin,' Tuck had said. 'The word *servus*. It means slave.'

It meant more than a single word to Edward. It meant having to work the land that belonged to the local lord before he was allowed to work on his own croft or strip of field. It meant that although he lived on the edge of a forest more than thirty miles square, he was not allowed even to collect brushwood to light a fire. It meant little food at the best of times and famine and disease at the worst. And it meant living in fear of terrible punishments for tiny offences: a heavy fine for grinding his own corn, a whipping if he spoke insolently to his lord, the loss of a hand if he snared so much as a single rabbit.

And yet there had been a time when Edward had thought that perhaps things might change – that perhaps one day he might be a serf no more. Robin Hood had brought him that hope. He had lost it for ever almost exactly one year ago.

He was in a bitter mood now, and it showed as he greeted the visitor with a muttered 'Good morning, my lord.'

Robert looked at the man – grey-haired and bearded, dressed in a simple, rough tunic, with no shoes on his feet. He sensed the villager's hostility, but ignored it. 'This is the village of Wickham?' he asked.

'Ay, my lord,' Edward replied. 'Not much of a place, as you can see.' He rubbed his calloused hands together. He had spent hours working on his vegetable patch – and for what? A handful of peas and parsley. But this young stripling – he would dine on venison that night. And he wouldn't have to work to earn it. 'What can I do for you, my lord?' he asked.

'We have to talk.'

'My lord?'

Robert got down from his horse and moved closer to Edward so that only he could hear. 'I've come from Herne,' he said.

Edward smiled slowly and mirthlessly. Herne the Hunter had not been seen or heard of for a year now. He had not come to the village since the time of the Blessing, a feast that had taken place when Robin Hood, Herne's son, was still alive. And now, to hear Herne's name on this stranger's lips ... it had to be some sort of a trick.

'Herne is a spirit, my lord,' Edward said.

'And his son?' Robert countered. 'The hooded man. Is he a spirit too?'

Edward paused. This was dangerous talk. Then he smiled

as if he had just realized that his leg was being pulled. 'My lord must be making some sort of joke!' he exclaimed. 'All this talk of Herne and hooded men! Why, it's beyond me and that's the truth.'

Robert hesitated. So Edward didn't trust him. And if he didn't trust him, he wouldn't help him. But the village of Wickham *had* to be where his quest began. What had Herne said to him? 'In the past lies what is to come.' The past ... one year ago ... Wickham.

'Inside,' he said.

Followed by an astonished Edward, he walked into one of the village huts. It was empty now, the sunlight streaming in through the circular hole in the wall that was the window. But Robert remembered it as it had been when Herne had called him to rescue the outlaws, when he had taken on the mantle of the hooded man.

'A year ago,' he said. 'Remember? Scarlet was sitting there – against the wall. Little John was next to him. Nasir was over there by the door. And you were here too, weren't you – the Sheriff's prisoner?' Edward started and Robert smiled. 'Yes.' He pointed. 'You were over there. "They have my son," you said. So I left you here. The others I cut free.'

Edward's mouth had fallen open. 'You!' he whispered. 'The hooded man!'

Robert nodded. 'Where are they now?' he asked. 'I've got to find them.'

'They've gone.' Edward stared at the nobleman as if he were dreaming. 'They lost heart,' he continued. 'Some say there was a quarrel. Tuck's the only one left. But he's deep in Sherwood now.'

'Could I find him?'

'The children know where he is.'

Edward gestured towards the door as if to go in search of some of the village children, but then he froze. A second horseman had ridden into Wickham and was now examining Robert's horse, tethered outside the mill. Edward recognized the horseman at once.

'Gisburne!' he hissed.

'Get rid of him,' Robert whispered.

At once Edward left the house, bowing his head as he approached Guy of Gisburne. The Sheriff's steward had arrived in Wickham by chance – but it was a route that he often took. He enjoyed lording it over the villagers and he was always on the look-out for trouble. He had spotted the horse at once. It obviously belonged to a nobleman. The villagers could never have afforded such a fine animal: perhaps one of them had stolen it. Gisburne hoped so. He hadn't enjoyed a good hanging for at least a week.

'Whose horse is this?' he demanded, seeing Edward.

'We don't know, my lord,' Edward said, touching his forelock. Even if he didn't feel like a serf, he could still play one when he needed to. 'We reckon it threw its rider. We've men out looking for him now.'

Gisburne looked at the horse appreciatively. 'A nobleman's horse,' he muttered, his eyes narrowed. 'But a nobleman with a longbow.'

Edward glanced at the grey's saddle and felt his heart lurch. There was a bow and a quiver of arrows strapped at the side – and he would have recognized them anywhere. Another man had carried a bow just like it once, a hooded man. These weapons had come from Herne.

'Yes, my lord,' he murmured. 'I thought that was odd myself.' He gave Gisburne a village idiot's grin. 'Not a knight's weapon is it, my lord!'

'I've seen it before,' Gisburne muttered.

'The longbow, my lord?'

'The horse!' There were few things in life that Gisburne enjoyed, but riding was one of them and he remembered horses the way a glutton might remember a good meal. 'I've seen it before,' he repeated. 'But where?'

'We'll solve that for you, my lord, when we find the owner.' Edward was still grinning madly, desperately hoping Gisburne would leave. If he found Robert there in the village, who knew what might happen?

Gisburne thought for a minute, trying to place the horse. A big grey, of fine stock ... but where? Then he swung his own horse round. The Sheriff was waiting for him in Nottingham – and the Sheriff didn't like to be kept waiting too long.

'Find the owner,' he snapped. 'Or bring the horse to me in Nottingham.' Then he rode away.

There was a feast that night in Wickham village. To honour Robert of Huntingdon a pig was killed so that for once the villagers could dine on meat. There were fresh loaves of barley bread, cheese and curds, ripe apples and oatmeal cake – all washed down with frothing jugs of mead.

Robert of Huntingdon was no longer dressed in the fine clothes of the castle. The following morning he was to enter Sherwood Forest again and that was no place for bright colours or delicate materials. Now he was dressed in a dark green tunic, made of leather and ringed with loops of metal. Edward had found the clothes for him in a great chest that he kept hidden beneath his bed.

Once, those clothes had been made for Robin Hood. Only Robin's magical sword, Albion, was missing from the broad leather belt. For that now belonged to Marion.

So they feasted, and as the moon sailed above Wickham and the stars glimmered in the night sky, Edward smiled at Robert and the spark of hope that he had once felt flickered again.

'Good luck to you, Robert of Huntingdon,' he said.

'No,' Robert shook his head, 'not of Huntingdon. That life is over.'

'Robert of Sherwood,' Edward said.

Robert turned to face the villagers crowded around the table. He was holding a bowl of mead. Slowly he lifted it.

'Herne protect us,' he said.

'Herne protect us,' the villagers chorused.

And somewhere, far away, Herne the Hunter heard the words and raised his hands to send his blessing through the forest, silent beneath the stars, carried by the wind that whispered its way into the village of Wickham.

7. FRIAR TUCK

'Tuck!'

Two children from the village had led Robert into Sherwood, but now he was alone. This was the area where the friar had last been seen – Friar Tuck, the only one of the outlaws who had remained in the forest after the death of Robin Hood. There was no sign of him now, but following a bubbling stream through the undergrowth, Robert came upon two loaves and three fish on the ground. He smiled to himself. The fish were lying on a piece of sackcloth and glistening in the sunlight. Gingerly he picked one up. A single dead eye stared beadily at him. The fish had been caught only in the last few minutes – and there was the rod that had caught it, a branch cut from a tree with a string and a hook attached, poking out of a bush a few yards away.

It was only when he had reached it that Robert realized that the makeshift fishing-rod was balanced on a stone without the fisherman at its end. So where was Tuck? The answer came a moment later as a roughly spherical figure charged forward with all the cunning and finesse of a herd of stampeding horses. Robert stepped aside. The figure, swinging a club and now running too fast to stop, hurtled past and dived into the water, disappearing with a massive splash.

Robert could hardly stop himself laughing as Friar Tuck surfaced, spitting water, a piece of green slime lodged on his bald pate.

'Forgive me!' the friar spluttered as he trod water. 'Forgive me. I mistook you for an enemy. I thought you were someone else.'

Tuck propelled himself towards the bank of the stream,

which was evidently deeper than Robert had first thought. 'Help me!' The friar reached out with one hand.

Still smiling, Robert reached down to pull him ashore. Their hands met and then the smile vanished from Robert's face as he felt himself jerked off his feet, arching through the air and into the water. The next moment, Friar Tuck was on top of him. It was like being strangled by a whale. And the water was freezing.

'Tuck!' Robert shouted while the friar grabbed him in a bear-hug that would have made a bear seem tame by comparison. 'Listen to me! I'm from Ed . . .' The sentence was abruptly cut off as Robert was forced underwater. Then, somehow, he managed to break free. He got to the surface, gasped at the air, and began again. 'I'm from Edward of Wickham. I'm a friend. The children . . .'

Once again the world vanished as he was forced into the chilly water. Friar Tuck was implacable. From a distance – in his robes – he could have been an old woman doing her washing. But it was Robert he was putting through the mangle. Robert realized that if he didn't do something soon, he'd drown . . . and even if he didn't drown, he'd probably end up with pneumonia. He twisted out of Tuck's grasp and kicked away, swimming underwater. Friar Tuck paused, searching through the water for a sight of him.

Then Robert surfaced behind the friar and clutched him round the neck. 'I need your help!' he shouted.

At last the message seemed to get through. 'Who are you?' Tuck asked.

The two men stood in the stream, Robert's arms clasped around Tuck's neck.

'I'm Robert of Huntingdon.'

'Robin of Huntingdon?'

'No – Robert. I'm the hooded man!'

'Oh yes!' Tuck smiled. 'And I'm the Archbishop of Canterbury!'

As he spoke, Tuck bent forward and for a second time Robert was sent in a dizzy somersault that was broken only by the cold slap of the water. But this time, as he soared over the friar's head, he managed to shout out three words.

'Marion's in danger!'

It was enough. He had no sooner hit the water than the friar had grabbed him again, dragging him to the bank. There they rested, the water dripping from their clothes. Robert was exhausted. As for Tuck, his face was bright red, his stomach rising and falling like a blacksmith's bellows.

'Let's have something to eat,' he said.

And they did. The fish that Robert had seen earlier made a good meal for two and Tuck had brought a skin of wine with him too. The friar drank greedily, and when he had taken his fill he rose.

'So it was you . . . the hooded man,' he said, passing Robert the wineskin.

'Yes.'

'And Herne chose you as his son?' Tuck nodded gravely. 'Why have you come here, Robert? Why now?'

Robert drank from the wineskin. He was sitting wrapped in a blanket beside a fire that Friar Tuck had built. The flames had dried him but still he shivered in the cool of the evening. Tuck was the first of Robin Hood's outlaws that he had met and, looking at him, as round as he was tall, his head tonsured, his lips sucking at a fish-bone, it seemed incredible that he had shared in so many adventures. And yet, despite his soaking in the stream, Robert liked him. It seemed impossible not to.

So now he told his story – how Owen had come to Huntingdon Castle, the dance with Marion and the abduction that had followed.

'Sir Richard of Leaford tried to get her back with soldiers hired from the Sheriff,' he explained. 'But the Sheriff tricked him. Afterwards, he wrote to my father.'

'And what did your father do?' Tuck asked.

'He blamed me.' Robert sighed. 'He said that if I hadn't angered Owen of Clun in the first place, none of this would have happened.'

'You don't believe that, do you?' Tuck snorted.

'No . . . maybe not.' Robert edged closer to the flames. 'But that was when I knew that I had to do something myself. I left Huntingdon the next morning . . . went to Herne. I won't be going back to the castle.'

There was a long silence. Friar Tuck poked at the flames, sending bright sparks spiralling up into the darkening sky. 'Hathersage,' he said. 'That's where John went. I'm sure of it. And Much went with him. But as for the others . . .'

'Hathersage,' Robert broke in. 'Will you come with me, Brother Tuck?'

Tuck looked at the young man who sat opposite him, his eyes dark pools of shadow behind the flames of the bonfire, his fair hair glowing red. Could this boy possibly bring the outlaws together again? Could he – could anyone – follow in the footsteps of Robin Hood?

And yet, for Tuck, the last year had been a wilderness time. He had lived in Sherwood Forest, poaching meat and catching fish, occasionally meeting up with the Wickham children to tell the old tales and breathe new life into the legend of Robin Hood. None of them even believed that he was dead, and that was the way Friar Tuck preferred it. But he had known. And he had never been more alone.

And now here was someone . . . someone who might just be able to turn time back, to make it all happen again.

'Will you come with me, Brother Tuck?'

Friar Tuck smiled sadly. 'I don't have any choice.'

They left the following morning before first light, riding together for Hathersage. It was still cold and Robert had drawn up his hood, covering his head. He rode the grey horse, taking the lead, while Friar Tuck followed on the bay that he had ridden in his days with Robin Hood.

Their departure was witnessed by a weasel-faced man, gap-toothed and unshaven. He had come to Sherwood Forest early for a purpose. He was setting traps, cruel wire snares that would torture before they killed. The man was a poacher. Once he had been caught by the soldiers of the Sheriff of

Nottingham. It should have cost him his hand, but that day the Sheriff had been in a merciful mood. He had allowed the poacher to remain free, provided he became an informer.

Now he watched carefully as the two figures passed. He heard the hooded man speak.

'There's still an hour to sunrise, Tuck,' he said. 'We'll sleep when we reach the moors.'

The poacher waited until the two men had turned a corner and disappeared from sight. He had recognized Friar Tuck. Only one man in the world could have a shape like that. The other man had been wearing a hood, but the poacher knew exactly who he was.

So the stories were true. Robin Hood hadn't died a year ago. Somehow he had tricked the Sheriff's men. And the poacher had just seen him ride past.

8. LITTLE JOHN

The wolf froze, its black eyes fixed on the flock of sheep grazing in the field five hundred yards away. A bead of saliva trickled out of the corner of its mouth and hung like a cobweb at its neck. It had been a week since it had fed on fresh mutton, but the dried blood still caked the fur around its snout. And now it was hungry again. Its tongue hung over its jagged teeth and its whole body trembled with desire. The wolf sensed danger, but ignored it in its greed. As if coming to a sudden decision, it pounced, leaping across the grass towards the unsuspecting sheep.

Much saw it before it had covered the first hundred yards. 'John!' he shouted.

A year ago he would have waited for Little John to come and sort out the trouble. But in the past twelve months Much had changed. He still looked the same – short and boyish with fair, curling hair – but there was a hardness about him that had set in the day Robin Hood had died. For Robin had died for him. He had been on the hill with Marion when the Sheriff's men had attacked. Robin had ordered them to go, staying behind to cover them. That was when he had been killed, and Much could never forget it.

Now he ran forward without waiting for Little John. His longbow was already in his hand and as he ran his other hand reached back to pull an arrow out of his quiver. The wolf had covered another hundred yards. In just seconds its teeth would be tearing at the throat of a baby lamb. Much loaded, aimed and fired without hesitating. The arrow sped across the field. The wolf howled, then crumpled in a ragged ball of fur, the shaft and feathers slanting out of its side.

'Well shot! You got him, Much! Well shot!'

Little John bounded up behind him and pounded his back with one mighty hand. Together they moved forward to the corpse of the wolf.

'He's eaten his last lamb,' John said. He nodded appreciatively. 'Worth a bit too.'

'Is he?' Much asked.

'Ay. The lord'll give us six pence for its head.'

'Six pennies for a wolf's head!'

Much had spoken the words before he realized what he had said. A wolf's head. It was another word for an outlaw. Once they had all been wolfsheads.

He glanced up at Little John. The big man had taken out his knife, but now he stood still and his eyes were far away. They had been shepherds for about a year now, working together in the wind-swept fields of Hathersage. But sometimes Much wondered if Little John had ever really left Sherwood Forest. If he had, he had left something of himself behind.

'Ay, a wolf's head,' Little John muttered, looking at the dead animal. 'Ours were worth more.'

The wind moaned softly. It was going to be another cold day.

'It was Robin Hood. I swear it.'

The poacher stood in the great hall of Nottingham Castle while Guy of Gisburne regarded him with cold disinterest. The poacher had thought that his knowledge – what he had seen that morning – would be worth money, a lot of money. But Sir Guy was cynical. And the Sheriff, busily tasting a batch of new wine that had just arrived at the castle, seemed hardly aware that he was there.

'Did you see his face?' Gisburne demanded.

'He was wearing a hood,' the poacher admitted. 'But he was talking. I heard him. "Tuck," he said, "we'll sleep when we get to the moors." I heard him.'

'Anything else?'

'No.' The poacher thought for a moment. 'He was on a grey and Tuck was riding a big bay. Heading north they were, on the Hathersage road.' He glanced from Gisburne to the Sheriff and back again. 'It was Robin Hood, I tell you!' he pleaded.

Gisburne was thoughtful. Nothing the poacher had said had made any sense ... not until he had mentioned one small detail. Perhaps it was just a coincidence, but he had seen a grey horse only a short time before. The horse of a nobleman, but equipped with a longbow, the weapon of a peasant. That was a mystery in itself. What had the horse been doing in Wickham? Could someone be stirring up old ghosts, impersonating Robin Hood?

Meanwhile, the Sheriff was tasting another cask of wine. He sipped a mouthful, screwed up his eyes and spat it out. The stuff was pure vinegar!

'Send it to the Abbot Hugo!' he rasped, wiping the taste away from his lips. 'For communion wine!'

A servant carried the offending cask away while another offered the Sheriff a taste from a further cask. The Sheriff took it, then walked slowly back towards the poacher. A silver penny had appeared in his hand as if by magic and now he tossed it to the man.

'Keep your eyes and ears open,' he commanded, 'and there might be more.'

It was a dismissal. The poacher bowed and left.

The Sheriff sipped his wine. This one was definitely better. Not fit for a man with his refined tastes, perhaps, but just about all right for guests. Perhaps the next time King John visited ...

'So who was the man with Tuck, Gisburne?' he asked, languidly.

'You'll find this hard to believe, my lord ...' Gisburne began.

'Very likely.'

'There was a grey horse in Wickham yesterday,' Gisburne continued, ignoring the barb. 'A horse of quality. They were looking for its owner in Sherwood ... they thought he had been thrown. At least, that was their story. This morning I remembered where I'd seen the animal before. I never forget a horse.'

The Sheriff yawned. 'I'm sure you don't.'

'It was on our visit to Huntingdon. It belonged to the Earl's son, Robert of Huntingdon.'

'So?'

Gisburne smiled. 'Your question was – who was the man with Tuck?'

The Sheriff considered, but only for a moment. He and Gisburne had a strange relationship. It was probably true to say that the steward disliked his master rather more than the master disliked his steward, but neither way was there much love lost between them. Gisburne had taken every opportunity to betray the Sheriff, even resorting to murder in his attempts to get away from the man. But owing to a combination of bad luck and sheer stupidity, none of his plots had ever succeeded. The Sheriff knew this. But it amused him to have Gisburne around, to tease and torment him and to take out his frustrations on him. As for Gisburne, he was bound in service to the Sheriff. It was as if he were the Sheriff's dog, given the freedom only of a short leash.

So when the Sheriff spoke, it was more to sneer at Gisburne than to reason with him. 'Tell me this,' he said. 'Why should Robert of Huntingdon, heir to vast estates and several castles, concern himself with a gang of outlaws?'

It was a good question but, for once in his life, Gisburne was ready with the answer. 'Marion of Leaford,' he said.

The Sheriff, sipping wine, choked and sent a fine red spray into the air. Sometimes the extent of Gisburne's idiocy surprised even him. And this time the steward's behaviour was more surprising still. Instead of sloping off and sulking, as he would normally have done, he held his ground.

'Let me track this man down, my lord,' he said, 'this hooded man. Let me find him for you. Then, maybe, you'll see ...'

The Sheriff stared at him. Gisburne was actually angry. He was convinced that he was right and he was angry because the Sheriff disagreed. The Sheriff was amazed, but he was also in a good mood. After all, at the end of the month he would have all the lands of Leaford, along with the Grange, to call his own. If Gisburne wanted a little holiday ...

'All right,' he said. 'If you really want to go traipsing off around the country ...'

Gisburne bowed and left. The door slammed shut behind him. The Sheriff of Nottingham drained his goblet and absent-mindedly held it out to a servant to be refilled.

'Robert of Huntingdon!' he muttered to himself. 'Really, Gisburne, sometimes you go too far!'

In Hathersage, Little John was sitting with Much beside his hut, stretching his legs after a hard day's work. The hut resembled a ruined church – which it might indeed once have been. Now it was little more than a pile of stones, perched on a hill at the edge of a desolate field. The hut offered little protection against the wind which moaned and whistled day and night across the wastes of Hathersage. Here, outside the friendlier surroundings of Sherwood Forest, it was always cold and wet. Though Much and Little John were well wrapped up in sheepskins, they were never really warm. The cold found its way into their clothes, seeped through their skin, circulated with their blood and chilled their very bones.

They were about to light a fire for their evening meal when Much saw the two travellers. The one lagging behind was easily recognizable, even at that distance.

'It's Tuck!' Much exclaimed.

'Ay,' Little John agreed. 'But who's that with him?'

Much held his hand up to his eyes, gazing at the figure silhouetted against the horizon. It was a strange time of day – neither day nor night but something in between. The sun had sunk behind the fields and would remain there for several hours. When night came, it would come suddenly, blotting out the world in inky blackness.

Much gazed at the figure, but he could not see who it was.

'For a moment,' he said, 'I thought ...' But he left the sentence unfinished, unwilling to press on old wounds.

'It means trouble, this does,' Little John growled. 'I can smell it.'

Together, Much and Little John walked down to greet the two riders. It was not the most friendly of greetings.

'You said you'd never leave Sherwood, Tuck,' Much said.

'Well I changed my mind,' Tuck replied as he got down from his horse – much to the poor beast's relief. He straightened his robes and glanced from Much to Little John. 'How are you?' he asked. 'It's good to see you.'

Little John ignored him. 'Who's this?'

'He's Robert of Huntingdon,' Tuck answered before Robert had a chance to speak for himself.

'What's he want with us?'

'Your help.'

This time it was Robert who had spoken. He was looking at Little John with a calm, almost emotionless face. He knew that he was going to have to proceed carefully. For even without his costly Huntingdon robes on, he was obviously a nobleman, maybe even a friend of the king ... and therefore certainly no friend of Little John's. Why should the big man trust him? He had never laboured in a field, a smithy or a mill. He had never been at the sharp end of an unjust lord's temper. He had never been cold and hungry, not in all his young life. The two men were complete opposites, and everything about Little John's manner screamed at him to turn and bolt for safety while he still could.

'It's Marion,' Tuck said. 'She's been captured by Lord Owen of Clun.'

'Has she?' Little John's eyes were still fixed on Robert.

'John!' Tuck insisted. 'You've got to ...'

'You're wasting your time,' Little John cut in. 'We're shepherds.'

Much nodded his agreement. Robert leant forward, once again choosing his words carefully. 'I saved you from the Sheriff,' he said.

'It's true,' Tuck added.

Little John scratched at his beard. 'So you were the hooded man, were you?'

'I was. I am.'

'Then why didn't you join us?' The words were as hard as the stones of the tumbledown shelter that had been John's home for a year.

'He's the son of the Earl of Huntingdon!' Tuck exclaimed. He could feel the trouble brewing, but there seemed to be nothing he could do to stop it.

'Is he?' Little John laughed briefly and without a trace of humour. 'Then he'd better get his father to rescue Marion.'

'Listen . . .' Robert began.

'No, you listen!' A whole year of rejection and resentment had been building up inside Little John's massive frame and now it all poured out. 'You're all the same, aren't you?' he cried. 'We saved Marion's father once. Did he join us? No! He bought his way back into favour with King John and Marion was pardoned. Were we pardoned? Did Sir Richard lift a finger to help us? Not likely! We're still looking over our shoulders, aren't we? Still outlaws. Still on the run. And you come here . . .'

'Wait!'

Robert was leaning forward, looking at Little John, desperately searching for something inside the man, something that John didn't even know was still there.

'You believed in Robin, didn't you,' he said.

'Ay.' Little John nodded slowly. 'That I did.'

'Why?'

For a moment Little John calmed down as he remembered. 'Because the fire burned bright in him,' he said, 'and for a time it warmed us all. But he's gone and the fire went with him. It's all over.'

'No,' Robert muttered.

And then Little John was angry again. 'How could you understand?' he demanded. 'You!' His voice was full of scorn. 'Ever starved? Ever been whipped because you forgot to lower your eyes when your masters rode by? Not you. Because you're one of them.'

Now it was Robert who lost his temper. He had left his home, forfeited his birthright, followed Herne, fought with Tuck and ridden miles through wind and rain . . . and Little John was treating him as if he were some sort of simpleton.

'Little John?' he muttered icily. 'Little Brain more like . . .'

Friar Tuck's eyebrows rose. Even Much shook his head in disbelief. Little John was almost seven feet tall and built like an ox. Nobody talked to him like that – nobody who wanted to stay alive.

'You'll pay for that,' Little John growled.

'No, John . . .' Tuck scolded.

Little John strode back to the shelter and picked up a thick rod, made of wood and about five and a half feet long: a quarter-staff. This was his favoured weapon and he was an expert with it. At the same time, Robert dismounted and unhooked his sword-belt, passing it to Friar Tuck. Much was holding a second quarter-staff and Robert took it from him, smiling as if the two of them had been good friends all their lives. Despite himself, Much was impressed. Just about anyone else he knew would have been white with fear – and that probably included himself. None the less, he had to demonstrate which side he was on.

'Go on, John!' he shouted. 'Teach him a lesson.'

Robert turned round, still smiling. He gripped Much's quarter-staff, ready for the first encounter. 'Come on, John,' he mocked. 'Teach me a lesson!'

Never again would Little John and Robert fight as they fought that day – and never would Much or Friar Tuck forget it. The shepherd was about a foot taller than the nobleman, several inches wider and several years older. He had used the quarter-staff all his life, while Robert's father would have been horrified to learn that his son had ever picked one up – for, like the longbow, it was hardly the weapon of a knight. And yet they were evenly matched. At least, that was the way it looked.

In the first encounter they tested each other's speed and strategy, exchanging a succession of blows that were so fast that they dazzled the eye and so furious that the clacking of wood against wood could be heard half a mile away. They paused, then set to again, this time searching for the vital opening in the other's defence that could lead to a cracked skull or – at best – a bruised shoulder. Next, Little John tried a different tactic, taking giant strides forward, the quarter-staff clutched in both hands, swinging it down like a long club. But Robert was ready for him. His own staff was held horizontally above his head, warding off the blows as he sprang back.

End of round one: stalemate.

Friar Tuck had moved round to stand beside Much and he watched the fight keenly. He had only known one other man who was the equal of Little John with the quarter-staff . . . a man it hurt him to put a name to. 'By heaven, he's good,' he whispered.

Much nodded, feeling something stirring inside him. It was a sense of excitement and of sheer pleasure . . . a sense of adventure that he had not felt for twelve long and tiring months.

Then the impossible happened.

Little John had changed his strategy once again, swinging low, aiming for Robert's ankles. The first time he had tried it, Robert had jumped and the staff had passed harmlessly beneath him. But when Little John attempted the move for a second time, Robert anticipated it and jumped early so that he was already up in the air as the quarter-staff whistled along the grass, and before Little John knew what had happened, he had landed on it with both feet, trapping it against the ground. Little John straightened up. He was unarmed, at Robert's mercy.

'Tricks, eh?' Little John breathed heavily, waiting for the blow from Robert's staff that would finish it.

But Robert had no wish to harm the big man. He stepped back, allowing Little John to pick up his weapon. Little John frowned. He had thought of Robert as no more than the offspring of a nobleman. But the boy had spirit. And he knew how to fight. None the less, Little John couldn't allow himself to be beaten ... and certainly not in front of the others.

He set to again and this time he used a trick of his own. The two quarter-staffs swung together and locked, forming a cross: Robert's held vertically, Little John's running horizontally. For a moment the two fighters remained in their positions. Then suddenly Little John slid his own staff down so that it caught Robert's fingers. Robert yelled in pain and surprise and dropped his own staff. At once Little John was covering him, daring him to make a move.

Now Robert was unarmed. The tables had been turned.

For perhaps one second Little John was tempted to knock the Earl's son clean into the next world. But despite his fearsome appearance, he was a kind and gentle man. More to the point, he was a good sport. Robert had given him a chance and he would return the compliment. He dug the end of his staff under Robert's, then flicked it. Robert's staff flew through the air, and Robert caught it.

The two men faced each other wearily.

But then Friar Tuck came between them. 'That's enough!' he said, firmly. He stared at them with all the authority of the thirteenth-century church, daring them to defy him. Little John gazed darkly at him, then threw down his weapon and stormed into the shelter. Much shrugged apologetically, unsure quite what to say. Robert hesitated for a moment, then followed the shepherd into the ruined building.

He found Little John sitting on the floor, his face filled with a sadness that had come to him with the force of a physical pain. 'Leave us in peace!' he muttered with a thick voice.

Robert knelt down beside him. 'Ever since I can remember,' he said, quietly, 'my father told me that one day I'd become the Earl of Huntingdon. That was my destiny, my duty.' He took a deep breath. 'Do you understand?' Little John made no answer, so he went on. 'When Robin died, Herne chose me to take his place.'

'No one can take his place.' The tears were shining in the big man's eyes.

'That's what I believed. And that was why I couldn't do it ... even though I saw injustice everywhere. I lacked the courage.' Robert sighed. 'Then Marion came to Huntingdon. She was pale and lost ... and her heart was broken. But whatever you think, John, she's still one of you.'

There was a long silence broken only by the wind that still moaned around the shelter, whistling in through the door and tugging at their clothes and hair. At last Little John spoke.

'You're not the only one who lacked courage,' he said. 'I reckon we all did.' He shook his head and for the first time the beginnings of a smile flickered on his lips. 'I've tried to go back to what I was ... a shepherd. But you can't go back. Not in your heart.' He sniffed loudly and wiped a grimy hand across his eyes. 'Where did you learn to use a quarter-staff?' he asked.

Now it was Robert's turn to smile. 'One of the guards taught me,' he replied. 'At my father's castle.'

'Well ...' Little John nodded. 'He didn't teach you too badly.'

There was another silence. The two men had fought, but in that fight they had learnt more about each other than they could have in a week of conversation.

'So ... are you with me?' Robert asked.

Little John stretched out a hand. 'I'm with you,' he said.

9. DEPARTURE

The following morning, Little John ate his last breakfast at the ruined church in Hathersage. It was nothing more than a bowl of nuts which he shared with the three others, but it would last them until they had time to cook a proper meal.

'What about Scarlet?' Robert was asking.

'He'll take a bit of finding,' Much muttered.

Little John pondered. 'He told me once he had a brother. Ran an alehouse somewhere, he said. He could have gone there. Only trouble is, I've forgotten where it was.'

'London?' Robert suggested.

'No, not London.' Little John pondered again. 'Began with an L, though.'

'Lincoln?' Robert tried. 'Leicester?'

'No . . . it weren't either of them. It could have been York.'

'That's not an L,' Tuck scowled.

'I know it isn't,' Little John retorted. 'Anyway, what does it matter? I doubt he'd join us – not after the quarrel we had.'

Friar Tuck thought back. Nothing had seemed to go right after the death of Robin Hood. For a short time the outlaws had remained together, but it hadn't worked. One disastrous raid had followed another. They'd been lucky to escape with their lives. And suddenly they had realized that it was over. They had almost come to blows one night and the next morning Will Scarlet had gone. He hadn't told anyone where he was heading.

'Lichfield!' Little John exclaimed.

'Eh?' Tuck was dragged back into the present.

'Lichfield! That's where Scarlet's brother lives. I said it began with L.'

'Ay!' Tuck nodded. 'And if I know Scarlet, it'll end with 'ell too.'

At Clun Castle, Marion was sitting silently on her bed. She had lost weight since her arrival at the home of the Marcher lord, barely managing to force down even the smallest amounts of food. Once, a long time ago, she might have found the strength to fight back. Had she thought that there was anybody in the world who could rescue her, anyone outside the castle who might even be thinking of her, then she would have fought Owen tooth and nail. As it was, she could offer only passive resistance, sitting silent and immobile and drawing at least some solace from the knowledge that this behaviour enraged him as much as anything.

'Why don't you speak?' he roared at her. 'You're to be my wife! My wife! Wife to Owen of the House of Clun. You're going to bear my children, give me sons! And yet you crouch there like a captured hind! Look at me!'

Furiously, he grabbed hold of her. She made no move to stop him. She didn't even try to slap him as she had done that evening in Huntingdon Castle. When he released her at last, she fell back, sobbing, on to the bed. Owen looked at her with disgust. Then he strode out of her chamber, slamming the door behind him with a resounding crash.

His rage carried him down the corridor and through an archway at the far end. But here he paused and recollected himself. For this was the threshold of the great chamber occupied by Gulnar. And somehow, in the sorcerer's chamber, it was better to keep human emotions like anger, lust and pride under control lest they somehow find their way into Gulnar's spells.

The bald and evil sorcerer was there, chanting softly over a bubbling cauldron. Suspended on a metal grid was a small, black bottle. The heat from the liquid, glowing a deadly green, curled upwards, saturating the bottle. Two skulls watched the sorcerer with grinning teeth and hollow eyes. Not for the first time, Owen was struck by how much they resembled Gulnar himself.

'Incada anag rham
Ridor erin bach!'

The words, sung in that queer, strangled voice, made no sense to Owen but still he watched, fascinated.

'The feast of Arrianrhod is in three days,' Gulnar muttered, seeing his master standing by. 'Then you will wed the girl and this will make her ... more than willing.'

As he spoke, he clutched the metal grid, still red hot from the flames of the cauldron. But he showed no pain. His fingers were unmarked. With a ghastly smile, he swung it round so that Owen could take the flask. 'More than willing.' Owen felt a surge of triumph. The love-potion that Gulnar had prepared would turn the weeping girl into a wife worthy of him. How he longed for the feast of Arrianrhod!

A shadow fell across his face. Owen looked up sharply. Gulnar was holding the metal grid in front of the light so that a criss-cross pattern showed vivid on Owen's cheek. He stared at it with wild, bulging eyes.

'What do you see?' Owen hissed.

But Gulnar turned away. 'Nothing,' he replied, keeping the vision of violent and bloody death a secret for his own personal amusement.

'There! That's it!'

Little John had taken the last of his possessions from the house and tied them to his horse. Now he brushed his hands against each other and turned round to face Much. 'Look,' he said, 'if ... for any reason ... if we don't come back, you'll find twenty-seven pennies buried beneath the threshold.'

Much stared at his friend angrily. 'Keep 'em!' he cried. 'I'm coming with you.'

'No, lad.' Little John shook his head. 'You're not.'

'Don't call me "lad". I'm coming!'

Little John turned his back on Much and walked out of the shelter. He was quite convinced that he was making a one-way journey. Even assuming they could find Will Scarlet, walking into the castle of this Owen of Clun would be suicide. What could four of them do against four hundred? Well, he had promised Robert that he would come – and that was it.

As he tightened the saddle of his horse, he became aware of Friar Tuck standing beside him.

'He's a man now, John,' Tuck said.

'He's staying here!' Little John replied in a voice that would brook no argument.

But an argument was just what he got. For Friar Tuck was right. It was as if Much had grown five years in the last twelve months. The days when he could be treated like a child were behind him.

'I'm coming,' he insisted. 'And don't try to stop me, John. I've as much right to be part of this as any of you. Robin died for Marion *and* me.'

'*Robin died*.' It was the first time that either of them had ever admitted as much – at least not to each other. Robin's death had always been with them in Hathersage, but they had never talked of it. They had blotted it out of their minds until in a strange way it had grown to become a barrier between them. And Much had just smashed that barrier.

'He's right,' Tuck muttered.

Little John sighed. 'Ay. Get your horse,' he said.

And so it was that the four of them left Hathersage: Robert first, Tuck behind and Little John and Much bringing up the rear. Little John's sheep had been herded round to another shepherd and the fields were empty, the wild grass waving in the endless breeze. A stretch of pink rippled through the sky and in the far distance, on the very edge of the world, the clouds rolled and twisted as if struggling to break free of one another. Later there would be a storm. The thunder threatened softly in the air and the rays of the morning shimmered with a hard light.

The four riders were watched as they set off for Lichfield.

Sir Guy of Gisburne, riding a swift black horse, had followed the hooded man to Hathersage, arriving just in time to see them go. Now he cursed the fact that he was too far away to see the man's face. Friar Tuck and Little John – they were easily recognizable. The third rider was probably the miller's son . . . what was his name? Much. But who was leading them? Who was the hooded man?

Gisburne reined his horse forward. He would have to keep his distance, but he would follow them. As soon as they stopped, he would catch up with them. And then, at last, they would have their reckoning.

10. WILL SCARLET

The inhabitants of Lichfield would never forget the day the four travellers came.

They came in on one of the two Roman roads that met in what was now the main square. But for the chance meeting of these roads, no village would ever have sprung up there, gradually to develop into a busy market town. Lichfield looked even busier than it really was. The tall, gabled houses were packed tightly together with not an inch between them and the streets were filled with people shouting angrily at one another to make themselves heard above the general din.

But much of this was an illusion. The fronts of the houses concealed large, open gardens and courtyards behind, for the inhabitants of Lichfield – as in every town – grew many of their own vegetables and even kept animals. As for all the shouting, it was in truth good-hearted, part of the daily ritual. For outside the market, where the prices were fixed, the housewives delighted in bargaining. Even the price of a side of beef in the butcher's shop might well come down a few pence after twenty minutes' banter.

It must be said that Lichfield was not an altogether agreeable place. For a start, it stank – with raw sewage running free in the streets. Occasionally old crones appeared on the second floor of their homes only to throw buckets of slops out on to the pavement – without even looking to see who might be passing below. And why should they? They owned the pavement along with the house and it was your fault if you happened to be standing on it at the wrong time.

The butchers added to the filth, slaughtering their chickens outside their shops and splattering the street with blood. Black flies bothered and buzzed around everyone and everything.

Pigs scavenged freely, pushing through the pedestrians, their snouts eternally pressed to the ground. Only the pigs could drink from the town well, whose water would surely have killed any human being. Some of the richer traders, walking through Lichfield, did so with perfumed handkerchiefs pressed against their faces. The rest just put up with the stench – or had become so used to it that they no longer noticed it.

The travellers arrived in the morning when they were less likely to be noticed. Nothing moved at night in Lichfield, the people keeping to their homes during the hours of curfew. Ever fearful of attack, they lived behind locks and bolts while the watch patrolled the streets until dawn, pouncing on any strangers and, if they couldn't give a good reason for their presence there, carting them off to gaol.

But in the morning it was different. Nobody even looked twice as the travellers dismounted and walked in the direction of the Scathelock tavern. Scathelock was Scarlet's true name. He had changed it after the murder of his wife . . . long before he had met Robin Hood. He had chosen the name well. Scarlet was the colour of danger and the colour of anger. Will Scarlet was angry – and his anger made him dangerous.

The tavern was half-way down the street between a draper's and a dyer's. Robert tied his horse to a rail and went in, closely followed by his three friends. At first it was difficult to see anything inside, for the building was so full of smoke from an open fire that his eyes watered. Gradually, however, he made out about two dozen men, some sprawled unconscious on wooden trestle-tables, some throwing dice, some talking in low, secretive voices – all either drinking or drunk.

The babble of voices faded and stopped as Robert walked in. Heads turned in his direction.

'Scathelock!' he called out.

A figure detached itself from a group of people and turned to face him, leaning against a pillar that supported the arched roof. Little John's eyebrows rose. It wasn't difficult to tell that this man was the owner of the tavern. Short and on the fat side with broad shoulders, a thick neck and suspicious, hostile eyes, he was the spitting image of his brother. But for the fact that his hair was longer and he was wearing an apron, he could have been Will Scarlet himself.

'What do you want?' he demanded.

'Where's Will?' Little John asked.

'Who wants to know?'

'We're friends of his.'

'So?' The tavern-keeper shrugged unhelpfully.

Little John took a deep breath, trying to control his rising anger. 'D'you know where he is?' he said.

'Should I?'

'You're his brother.'

The brother, whose name was Amos Scathelock, sneered. 'What if I am?'

'Now look, friend . . .' Little John growled.

'No.' Amos smiled unpleasantly. 'You look . . . friend. Go on, look all you want. Can you see him?' Little John glanced around him and shook his head. 'Then he ain't here, is he, *friend*! So on your way . . .'

Little John clenched his fists in fury. This Amos Scathelock really was like his brother! At the same moment, Robert stepped forward. He was half the big man's size and several years his junior, but when he spoke it was with such quiet menace that he seemed somehow twice as dangerous.

'He's here,' Robert said.

Amos stared at him uncertainly. 'Are you calling me a liar?' he muttered.

'Not yet. Fetch him!'

'I won't stand for . . .'

Amos had begun to bluster, but Robert wasn't impressed. 'Fetch him!' he snapped.

At that moment a door crashed open at the side of the tavern. A ray streamed in . . . a ray of sunlight that imprisoned a million swirling specks of dust. A man stood silhouetted against it. For a few seonds he paused, taking in the scene, then slowly, deliberately, he walked in, picked up a mug of ale and drank it. Only half the liquid went into his mouth. The rest trickled out of the corners, down his neck and on to his chest.

Will Scarlet.

'I'm here,' he rasped, wiping the froth from his lips. Will was half-drunk. But he had been half-drunk for so long that he no longer noticed it. He moved closer to Robert. 'And who might you be?' he asked.

'Herne's son,' Robert said.

It was as if Will had been jabbed with a thorn. Although he tried to show no emotion, something flickered in his eyes, something that was very close to pain. Then he stretched out one hand, handing his brother the empty mug.

'I'll have another,' he said.

Amos took the mug.

Robert opened his mouth to speak.

Then Will hit him, hard, back-handed across the face. It was a savage blow, and all the worse for being completely unexpected. Robert was thrown off his feet and crashed into a table.

'I'll kill you!' Will Scarlet roared, a year of frustration and pent-up anger exploding inside him. Amos had refilled his mug. As Much helped Robert to his feet and half-carried him out of the room, he drank again.

It was then that Sir Guy of Gisburne arrived in Lichfield. He had followed the four riders all the way from Hathersage, but never once had he got close enough to see the face of the hooded man. Once the sun had caught a lock of fair hair and he had thought again of Robert of Huntingdon. But he had to get closer, prove it beyond any possible doubt. Only that way would the Sheriff be satisfied.

Now he saw the grey horse tethered outside the tavern – the same grey horse that he had seen in Wickham. So the outlaws must be inside! Should he go in? Gisburne thought about it, then decided against it. If the outlaws saw him, they would kill him for sure. Better to get help. There had to be a Sheriff's sergeant somewhere in Lichfield. He would rouse the watch and come back. And when he rode back to

Nottingham, he would take with him a prisoner. A hooded man . . .

By this time, Robert of Huntingdon was also a very bruised man. He had washed his face at the tavern's well and checked to make sure that all his teeth were still in place (they were), but the skin on the side of his face where Will had hit him was already puffy and sore.

'What are you going to do now?' Much asked.

'Persuade him,' Robert said.

'How?'

Robert took off his sword-belt and handed it to Much. 'Well, I've tried talking . . .' He strode purposefully back into the tavern.

Will Scarlet was downing a third mug of ale when Robert reached him. He just had time to frown in puzzlement when Robert hit him, sending him sprawling against a pile of barrels. Will lay there astonished. When he knocked people down they normally stayed down. This was different; this was an outrage. His brother appeared behind him and poured a jug of beer over his head, reviving him. With a low groan, Will got to his feet . . . and charged.

He charged like a bull, his head slamming into Robert's chest and carrying him with him out of the tavern and into the street. In a confusion of whirling arms and legs the two of them grappled together, rolling over and over in the dirt and straw. Then Scarlet was on top, dragging Robert to his feet only to knock him down again. But still Robert wouldn't stay down. As the other outlaws watched from the door of the tavern, he managed to head-butt Scarlet in the stomach, then weighed in with his fists, giving as good as he got.

Meanwhile the tavern had emptied and all work had stopped near by as the people crowded round to watch the fight. Four men, friends of Amos, had climbed on to a raised platform to get a better view. They loved a fight, as their own broken noses and missing teeth showed. And what better than somebody else's fight for a bit of painless entertainment? They leaned forward, shouting.

'Hit him!'

'Break him!'

'Bruise him!'

'Bite him!'

'Kill him!'

Thrown to the ground, Will Scarlet stared up at these four leering faces.

'Get up and fight!' they crowed.

Robert closed in but Will held up his hand. The crowd roared. It looked as if the great Will Scarlet had given in – and to a mere boy!

Will Scarlet got slowly to his feet.

'Get on with it!' the four men on the platform shouted.

'Get in there!'

'Get moving!'

Will lashed out. His foot caught the strut that held up the platform. The laughter and shouting abruptly turned into howls of fear as the four men and the entire platform plunged to the ground in an eruption of shattering wood. While Robert watched, hardly believing what he was seeing, Scarlet then proceeded to kick every one of the four men until they screamed for mercy. It seemed almost as if Will had forgotten just who he was meant to be fighting.

But not for long. When Scarlet strolled back to Robert, leaving four very battered spectators spread-eagled in the dirt behind him, he was smiling almost amicably. Then . . . *thwack*! Robert shot backwards into a herd of goats as Scarlet's fist caught him clean on the side of the jaw. Shaking his head, he got up and – as the crowd thundered its applause – threw himself on Will. The two crashed into the draper's stall. The draper leaned over the wooden counter, then disappeared altogether as the weight of the two men sent the counter flying upwards, breaking the wood in three places and the draper's nose in two.

It was the dyer's turn next. A whole row of recently dyed sheets hung outside his shop, bright red and white. As his wife screeched and he laughed, Will and Robert managed to get themselves tied up in the flapping material, punching at each other through the sheets. The dyer laughed again as Robert's fist buried itself in Will Scarlet's paunch. He laughed again as Robert kneed Will in the groin. And he was still laughing when Will's hand caught him on the shoulder, tipping him over backwards into a huge vat of red dye. When he emerged spluttering, he was red from tip to toe, and so he would remain for many months to come. 'He always did make me see red,' Amos muttered.

By now a huge crowd had gathered to watch the fight. Most days were the same in Lichfield, but this was a real piece of entertainment. Even the other outlaws were more amused than alarmed. If Will Scarlet had something he wanted to get out of his system, it was best he do it now and in the only way he could. And Robert was more than holding his own against him. It was an even contest. And – like the fight with Little John – in many ways it was a necessary one.

Robert and Will were tiring. Each had taken about as much as the human body can take without keeling over. They were backing down the main street of Lichfield, each one waiting for the other to make a move. That was when the town carpenter made his mistake.

He was a grey-haired, round-faced man who always smelt strangely of kippers and he had been watching the fight from the balcony of the second floor of his house. He was also holding a bucket of dirty water, and as Scarlet passed underneath, he upturned it. The crowd roared with laughter as Will was drenched, two cabbage leaves lodging themselves on his head.

Then the laughter died away as he looked up.

Will Scarlet was livid. His eyes promised death. Almost as an afterthought, he gave Robert a right hook that spun him into a market stall. Then, as the wretched carpenter gulped and wished himself a thousand miles away from Lichfield, he stormed up the steps that led to the balcony. The carpenter tried to get away, but Will was on him, slapping and smacking and finally taking the unfortunate man in his arms for a short dance that took them smashing through the balcony railing and down through the roof of a neighbouring barn. A dozen chickens squawked and screeched as Will dragged the carpenter out, holding him by the scruff of the neck.

'*Never* do that again!' he said.

He let the man go. The carpenter crumpled in a sad little heap at his feet. Then Will was off, searching for Robert, intent on finishing the fight.

He found him in the courtyard behind the tavern. Robert was sitting on a step, drinking a mug of beer. His clothes were caked with mud, his hair was dripping wet and his face was a mosaic of cuts and bruises, but as Will joined him he held out a second mug.

'I got you a drink,' he said.

Will took it and sat down on the step behind him. He drank heavily, then glanced down at Robert. 'I still don't like you,' he muttered.

Robert grinned. 'I'll drink to that.'

Will snatched up a pitcher of beer. 'Then have one on me,' he said and brought it down on Robert's head.

Robert shook beer out of his hair while Will Scarlet walked away. It was incredible. Everything the outlaws had told him about Will was true. He was unstoppable.

But Robert would stop him.

Taking a deep breath, he got to his feet and once again launched himself into the fray.

Gisburne had at last found the office of William Sparrow, the local Sheriff's sergeant. But he had not found much help. The sergeant was sitting behind a battlefield of a table where the instruments of his office – scrolls, parchments and quills – fought it out with goblets of beer and the remains of half-eaten meals. The room was a mess. So was the Sheriff's sergeant. A sallow-faced man with dark hair and darker eyes, he was slumped, half-asleep, in his chair, a profusion of red and white scarves knotted round his neck like some sort of crazy mayoral chain.

'Summon your men and follow me!' Gisburne exclaimed. 'I am Sir Guy of Gisburne.'

'I don't care who you are,' William Sparrow replied testily. 'You can't just burst in on the Sheriff's sergeant. That's not how we do things in Lichfield.'

He was not alone in the room. A clerk sat beside him, helping him count the bribes that he had taken that week. For like just about every Sheriff's sergeant in England, Sparrow was as corrupt as he was incompetent. The clerk was his brother. The other officers were cousins. The entire Sparrow family (right down to his grandmother who worked nights in the gaol) were very contentedly raking it in.

'There are five wanted men in Lichfield,' Gisburne exclaimed.

'Five?' Sparrow retorted. 'I'd have nothing to worry about if there were only five. Or only fifty-five . . .'

'These men are dangerous outlaws with a price on their heads,' Gisburne insisted.

By chance, Gisburne had used the one word likely to be of interest to the Sheriff's sergeant: price. If there was money involved, then perhaps action should be taken. But on the other hand, he had also used the word 'dangerous'.

'Ambrose!' Sparrow called out.

There was a pause. Then a gawky man with large ears appeared, stooping beneath a low doorway. 'Yes, cousin Sparrow?' he said.

'This is Sir Guy of Ginsborough,' Sparrow said.

'*Gisburne!*' Sir Guy exploded.

'Yes, well there's no need to shout, is there?' Sparrow sniffed. 'Where are these villains?'

'In the alehouse,' Gisburne said.

'That's Scathelock's place,' Ambrose muttered.

'I know it is.' William Sparrow poured himself a goblet of beer and drank it contentedly, watched by an increasingly angry Gisburne. He finished it and sighed. 'Scathelock makes the best ale in Lichfield,' he said.

Gisburne leant forward and looked the Sheriff's sergeant in the eye. 'I want you to arrest them,' he said.

'Arrest them? I don't even know them!'

'You've heard of Robin Hood, I suppose?' Gisburne asked icily. 'And Little John and Will Scarlet? Well – they're in Lichfield.'

'It's still daylight,' Sparrow said. He did at least know the law. 'They've every right to be.'

'They're wolfsheads!'

'In Nottingham. Not in Lichfield.'

There was no point arguing with Sparrow. Somehow managing to keep his temper under control, Gisburne tried another tack. 'Listen,' he said, quietly. 'They're worth thirty silver marks each.'

It worked. Sparrow glanced at the clerk. The clerk glanced at Gisburne.

'A hundred and fifty marks,' Gisburne continued, pressing home his advantage. 'Think of it.'

William Sparrow thought about it. They were making money every week. When the alewives were caught overcharging for their beer, for example. Or when the fishmongers tried to sell rotten fish. There were a hundred opportunities to extort a few pence here and there. But a hundred and fifty silver marks . . . !

'Ambrose!' he yelled.

'Yes, cousin Sparrow?' Ambrose was still standing in the room, a vacant smile on his face.

'Get the others,' the Sheriff's sergeant commanded.

The fight had found its way into the street behind the tavern when somebody shouted out that the watch was on its way. Neither Will nor Robert took any notice. They were barely able to stand up and swing punches that seemed to take an hour to arrive.

The watch, led by William Sparrow with Gisburne at his side, approached the tavern from the front. Ambrose and four other men followed, carrying an array of tools that must have been handed down from generation to generation for a hundred years. All in all they looked about as menacing as a chorus of nuns, but still Gisburne pressed on. He was vaguely aware that he had got himself into another ghastly mess, but he was still determined to make an arrest by hook or by crook – which, he reflected, glancing at the various weapons carried by the watch, was just about all he had.

He was greeted at the door of the tavern by Amos Scathe-lock. 'Where are they?' he demanded.

'Who?' Amos asked, all innocence.

'The outlaws!'

'What outlaws?' Amos turned to Sparrow whom he knew as a regular customer. 'Hello, William!' he said. 'What this about?' he pointed at Gisburne. 'Who's this?'

'Sir Guy of Gainsbone,' Sparrow said.

'*Gisburne!*' Gisburne screamed.

The watch marched into the now empty tavern and Gisburne stopped, drawing his sword. 'Search the place!' he commanded.

Sparrow looked at Amos. The smell of beer was thick in the air and he was already going off the whole idea, but now that he was here he might as well make a show of doing his job. He pointed at a large trap-door set in the floor. 'What's down there?' he asked.

'The cellar,' Amos replied.

'Open it up!' Sparrow demanded.

'There's no one down there,' Amos protested.

'Ambrose!' Sparrow exclaimed.

Ambrose sprang forward and with some difficulty managed to lever up the heavy trap-door. The six men peered into a large space, empty but for a clutter of empty barrels and a heap of filthy straw.

'He's right, cousin Sparrow,' Ambrose said.

Meanwhile, Little John had found Robert and Scarlet, picked them up and ducked their semi-conscious heads in the horse-trough. At the same time, Much and Friar Tuck had gone for the horses and even as Gisburne stormed out of the back of the tavern in search of them, they were mounting and preparing to leave. He arrived about thirty seconds too late. As he ran up a side alley, they galloped away down the main street. Robert's head was hidden from sight by the other riders and by the time Gisburne had run into the street, they were gone.

Furious and desperate, he ran back into the tavern, calling for the watch.

The trap-door was still open.

As the watch looked on, Gisburne tripped and disappeared head-first into it. There was a terrible clatter from the darkness below, then silence.

William Sparrow looked at his cousin reproachfully. 'You left the trap-door open, Ambrose,' he said.

Ambrose blushed. And closed it.

'Sorry about that, Ginsberg!' Sparrow called out.

And then they all went and had a beer.

11. THE BRIDE OF CLUN

Grim by day, Clun Castle was nothing less than deathly once the light began to fail and the evening set in. Then the stone walls would seem colder and greyer than ever. The guards, silently patrolling the passages, would become a little less human. And the torches, flickering against the walls, would create strange shadows, twisting shapes with a life of their own, dancing in the air like uninvited spirits of the night.

Nasir had been taken to the arena by the captain of the guard – a thin, pale man with long, jet-black hair. Grendal, as he was called, was the most prized of all Owen's soldiers. Like his master, he loved killing and but for the fact that he was needed to train new warriors for the blood game, he might well have ended up in the arena himself. For the past seven days he had been training Nasir with the ungainly weapons of the blood game. Now the two men faced each other for a final time.

Their swords clashed. Thrust, parry, block. A week before, Nasir had never held the heavy sword with the two spikes slanting up out of the hilt, but already he had become an expert with it. Grendal was beaten back, forced against the side of the ring, disarmed. Nasir raised his second sword for the kill . . .

'Enough!'

Owen of Clun stood above him, flanked by two guards, whose crossbows were levelled on the Saracen fighter. Nasir looked deep into the eyes of Grendal. The man was afraid of him and that was good. He lowered his swords.

'A killer, Grendal!' Owen's voice boomed out across the arena. 'A killer!' He grinned at Nasir, his teeth a fiendish white against his black beard. 'Win the blood game for me!' he cried.

'Tomorrow, at my marriage-feast!' Owen made as if to leave the arena, then turned back. 'Feed him well, Grendal,' he shouted. 'Plenty of red meat.'

Grendal gestured at a cage set in the wall of the arena. The two guards were still covering Nasir with their crossbows. There was nothing he could do: he allowed himself to be locked in.

'Keep on your toes and you'll win him a fortune,' Grendal said.

'Or die,' Nasir muttered.

The captain smiled. 'That's up to you.' He walked away, back across the arena, stopping to scoop up the swords.

Nasir watched him go. Tomorrow he would kill a man he had never even met. Then maybe another the week after that. And he would go on killing, Owen's champion, until the day it was his turn to die. He had no choice. He would never escape. For Nasir, the only escape would be death.

'*Who?*' Scarlet demanded.

'The Earl of Huntingdon,' Robert said.

'Your *father?*' Scarlet turned to the others in disbelief. 'And Herne's chosen *him?*'

Much and Little John nodded. 'Ay,' Tuck said.

Scarlet ran a hand through his hair. An earl's son? It wasn't possible. 'He must be right round the maypole,' he muttered.

The five men were resting in a clearing in the forest about twenty miles from Lichfield. Much had checked that they weren't being followed, while Friar Tuck had seen to the two fighters. In fact, despite appearances, they hadn't managed to hurt each other too badly. If anything, Will Scarlet had got the worst of it. But at least the fight had sobered him up. He was angry, irritable, unreasonable, unfriendly and unhelpful. In other words, he was very much back to his old self.

'You'll never get into Clun Castle,' he said now. 'And if you did, you'd never get out again.'

'We must,' Robert insisted.

'You don't understand, do you?' Will Scarlet moved forward to address the whole group. 'We ain't *sharp* any more,' he began. 'Not like we were. Look at us! Look at me. D'you think I couldn't have floored him if I hadn't been on the ale?' He jerked his head at Much and Little John who were standing together beside a tree. 'And you two. A year sitting on your bums watching sheep!' He gave a short, hard laugh and turned on Tuck who was sitting on the grass, his legs stretched out. 'And you, filling your belly with venison and sleeping most of the day ...'

Nobody spoke. There was a lot of truth in what Will was saying, though none of them would have wanted to admit it. Will looked out into the gloom and suddenly his expression changed. When he spoke again, his voice was softer, sadder. He was remembering ...

'We was as fast as wolves in Sherwood,' he said. 'They couldn't touch us. We could do anything, take on anyone. We've lost it.'

'*No, Scarlet. Nothing's forgotten. Nothing's ever forgotten.*'

Will's head snapped round. Robert was standing next to him. It was Robert who had spoken. 'What did you say?' he whispered.

'You heard me,' Robert said.

Scarlet shook his head slowly. Robert might have uttered the words, but it had been somebody else who had spoken. 'No,' he said. 'It wasn't you I heard.'

'Does it matter, Will?' Robert asked.

Will Scarlet leant against a tree, trying to arrange his thoughts. Herne's son ... a nobleman ... but he had fought like a true wolfshead ... and he spoke with the voice of ... the hooded man.

'It'd take a miracle to bring it off,' he said. 'Five of us.'

'Six – if we had Nasir,' Much muttered.

Scarlet gave him a condescending smile. 'But we haven't, have we?' he said.

'Where is he?' Robert asked.

'How should I know?' It was almost as if Scarlet were trying to start another fight. 'Back with his own people, if he's any sense. Or else he's a mercenary. Or dead.'

'Then we'll find others.'

Scarlet sighed. 'Not like Nasir.'

Robert looked at the four faces around him. Tuck, sitting gloomily on the ground; Scarlet, angry and impatient; Little John, willing to follow him anywhere; Much, trusting him so long as Little John did. It had cost him more bruises than he had suffered in his entire life – a trial by water, by quarter-staff and by fist – but somehow he had managed to bring them together. He couldn't spend any more time looking for Nasir, but he had done as Herne had told him.

'Find them. Bring them together.'

And now he would lead them ... to Clun Castle. Already the beginnings of a plan were forming in his mind. Tomorrow there was to be a full moon. That was when they would strike.

That same evening, Marion tried to escape.

The old crone who attended her brought the evening meal at the same time as she always did, carrying the food on a tray while a younger woman – possibly her daughter – waited by the door. Marion knew that the feast of Arrianrhod was to be held the next day. She knew that she had run out of time. So she acted.

As the tray was presented to her, she lifted off a plate of hot broth, and flung it into the old woman's face. The woman screamed and dropped the tray. At the same moment, Marion ran forward and pushed the daughter to one side. Then she dashed out into the passage, pulling the door shut behind her. The key had been left in the lock. She turned it and ran.

There was nobody in sight as she made her way down the gloomy passages of Clun Castle. The whole place seemed to be asleep. And yet something was astir. She could feel it. It was as if she were running along the filament of a vast spider's web and every move she made only served to alert the monstrous creature that lay somewhere above her, waiting to pounce.

A guard stepped out from behind a pillar, barring her way.

She froze, turned, tried to find another way out. A second guard appeared, his sword drawn. Then she saw Nasir. He saw her at the same moment and stretched one hand out between the bars of his cage.

'Nasir!'

'Marion!'

There was a soft chuckle from the end of the corridor. Somebody . . . something . . . passed beneath the archway and slithered towards her.

> *'Incada anag rham*
> *Ridor erin bach.'*

Gulnar sang the words softly. In one hand he held a human skull, its eye-sockets decorated with shining rubies. As he uttered his incantation, he gently swung the skull, smiling all the while. Marion found herself transfixed. The skull swung closer and closer. Now it filled her vision. All she could hear were the soft words repeated over and over again, boring through her brain and into the very heart of her consciousness. Closer and closer . . . the eyes were her eyes and she was the skull in Gulnar's hand. Slowly, she sank to her knees.

Gulnar set the skull down and took out the phial that he had shown Owen of Clun in his chamber. With long, bony fingers, he unfastened the top. Then he held it over Marion's head.

'Drink!' he commanded, a vein on the side of his bald head pulsating with excitement. 'Drink and your heart will burn with love-longing for the Lord of Clun!'

Marion stared up at him, her eyes blank. Gulnar tilted the bottle. Two drops of liquid dripped from the end of the phial, like blood from an open wound, and splashed on to her tongue.

'Drink!' he whispered.

For a minute he stared down at her while the potion took effect. Then he recoiled, his eyes bulging, a twisted smile threatening to crack his head in half. Marion's hands had stretched out to clasp the sorcerer passionately around the neck. Something wild flickered in her eyes.

'It is done!' Gulnar screeched. 'Let the women prepare her. For she is to be the bride of Clun!'

12. THE FEAST OF ARRIANRHOD

At last the feast of Arrianrhod had arrived and Clun Castle was filled with the sound of shouting and laughter. There had been a banquet. There had been minstrels and jugglers. All the old tales had been told . . . of women lost and battles won. But now the climax of the day was approaching. There was to be another blood game and – it was rumoured among the guests – Owen of Clun was to bet more money on his new champion than had ever been seen in the arena.

Owen stood there now, resplendent in a robe that formed a glittering tapestry of gold and silver across his back. It was the sort of robe that a priest might wear in the High Church, but on Owen the effect was purely devilish. His black hair and beard had been oiled and combed and he had taken a bath for the first time in a month. Then his face had been painted with a streak of pagan blue – the colour of the sky and the sky goddess Arrianrhod. The paint formed a band across his eyes, a backdrop against which the black pupils glimmered malevolently.

As his guests gathered around him, a hundred flaming torches filling the arena with smoke, he raised his goblet and called out:

'The Lord of Clun drinks to his wedding-guests!'

There was something very horrible about the guests. They were drunk and noisy with long straggling hair and wild eyes . . . but there was something more. They had come to a wedding, but they longed to see blood spilled. Like animals, they smelt it in the air. And the scent was driving them into a frenzy.

'Long life to Lord Owen!' they shouted. 'Long life!'

Owen held up a hand for silence. 'It is the feast of

Arrianrhod,' he cried. 'Tonight I become handfast to Marion of Leaford. And you shall bear witness to the marriage.'

'Long life to the Lord of Clun!' the wedding-guests chorused. 'And to his lady!'

For Marion had appeared ... if it was still Marion. She stood beneath an archway on the far side of the arena, dressed in a turquoise robe bound at the waist with a belt of solid gold. Her hair was loose, tumbling down to her neck where a golden torque of strange design hung about her throat. Golden bracelets snaked around her wrists. Her eyes had been painted in the same way as Owen's with a streak of primeval blue. But as she walked slowly into the arena past the staring guests, she was no longer Marion of Leaford. She was a creature enchanted, a puppet dangling on the invisible strings of the sorcerer Gulnar.

He was there too, waiting to greet her, his head hooded, a diamond-shaped brooch fastened to his forehead. In his hands he held two mistletoe branches, symbols of fertility, and as she walked towards him, he beat them together, the rustle of the leaves in time with her heart-beat.

'Hail to thee, Arrianrhod ...' Gulnar's voice sang out in the arena. He stood before his creation, his mad eyes gloating over her. '... Earth Goddess, Mother of Men. Be faithful in the embrace of the All-Father. Hail to thee, Marion! Kneel and worship thy lord!'

The mistletoe clashed above his head and Marion moved forward, her face filled with sudden desire, deep and barbaric. Gulnar followed her as she approached Owen.

'Hail to thee, Owen,' he gurgled. 'Take this woman as your wife!'

Marion stopped and knelt beside her lord and master. Then, having humbled herself, she stood and allowed herself to be swept into his embrace. It was hot in the arena. The wedding-guests were sweating. Owen pressed his lips against hers and this time she made no move to resist.

And there was Gulnar, the skin on his head stretched as

tight as a drum, ghoulishly watching as the wedding-guests cried out, over and over again:

'Hail to the Lord of Clun and to his lady!'

The feast of Arrianrhod had arrived.

The five guards stationed on the wind-swept hillside had a simple task. If a hostile army or raiding party should approach the castle, they would light a bonfire that had been built so that it could be seen for miles. A lit torch stood at the ready twenty-four hours a day and there was always someone stationed in the castle, watching out for the flames. But on this day, disgruntlement had made the guards careless. Their lord was being married and because they were on duty, they would miss the feast. To make up for it, they had managed to sneak a few wineskins out with them, and now they were drinking steadily, the wine warm in their bellies against the chill of the wind.

They never knew what hit them.

Robert of Huntingdon, Little John, Will Scarlet, Much and Friar Tuck had crept silently through the heather until the men were within range. Little John had spotted the guards and held up a hand with all his fingers forming a star. Five of them. The outlaws had loaded their bows. Robert gave the command.

'Now!'

Four arrows twanged through the air. Four men fell. Only Scarlet paused, waiting to get a clear aim on his target who was hidden behind a gorse thicket.

'You're aiming blind,' Robert said.

Scarlet fired. The fifth man jerked into sight with an arrow buried in his neck. He watched him fall to the ground and smiled. 'I know,' he muttered.

But it is difficult to kill a man instantaneously with an arrow fired through the wind from a distance of one hundred yards. Friar Tuck's arrow had wounded, not killed, one of the guards – who now managed to get to his feet and snatch the lit torch. At once Robert fired again, hitting the man in the heart. He died on his feet, but the torch fell into the bonfire, lighting the signal.

Robert sprang forward. The flames were still low, too low to be seen at the castle, but if they grew larger, if the alarm were raised, the outlaws would be beaten before they had even begun. Scooping up a piece of rag, Robert threw himself on to the fire, using his own body to smother the flames while he scattered the cinders with the rag. By the time the outlaws had reached him, the danger had passed. A wisp of smoke was all that remained of the fire. Little John clapped a hand on Robert's shoulder, genuinely impressed by his fast reaction.

'Warm work,' Robert muttered.

Twenty minutes later, he rode boldly up to Clun Castle. The main entrance – opposite the drawbridge that led over the moat – was barred by a huge portcullis. He reined in his horse in front of it and called imperiously to the guards.

'A messenger from King John,' he cried, in the voice of one used to being obeyed.

The guards did not hesitate. Robert's arrogant manner was enough.

'Take it up!' The head guard commanded.

One of the men ran into the gatehouse and began to turn the wheel that wound in the thick rope that raised the portcullis. Slowly, the gate slid upward, its jagged iron spikes pointing down to the ground like a line of daggers. As soon as the gate was open, Robert acted. A moment later the three remaining guards were unconscious ... two knocked out by Robert, the third shot by Much who appeared behind his horse. At the same time, Will Scarlet ran into the gatehouse. The guard who had been so obliging as to open the portcullis just had time to realize that something was wrong when a blow from a wooden club sent him to join his ancestors.

Meanwhile, Little John and Friar Tuck were crossing the moat at its shallowest point, carrying what looked like Scottish cabers. They were young trees, stripped of their leaves and branches and with the roots sawn off. The outlaws had prepared them the night before . . . for this was all part of Robert's plan.

While Much saw to the horses and Robert kept watch for any more guards, Friar Tuck and Little John positioned the tree-trunks under the portcullis.

'All right, Will!' Robert hissed.

Inside the gatehouse, Will Scarlet lowered the portcullis about six inches so that the teeth at the bottom jammed into the tops of the tree-trunks. Then he stepped back and slashed the rope with his sword. The portcullis was now open but supported only on the tree-trunks. Once the trunks were removed it would come crashing down and it would take a lot of men a lot of time to open it again.

Robert turned to Tuck. 'Right. Off you go,' he said.

'And don't be too long.' Little John straightened up holding a rope in each hand. Each rope had been tied round the foot of one of the tree-trunks. He tossed the other ends to Much, who was waiting with the horses outside the castle, below the level of the drawbridge.

'Come on!' Robert whispered.

Robert, Little John and Will Scarlet ran into the castle. Friar Tuck began the long journey back to the signal-bonfire. Much set about tying the ropes to the horses.

So far so good.

Led by Robert, the three outlaws passed from the barbican into the inner courtyard of Clun Castle. There was nobody in sight. An old fire smoked harmlessly in a metal brazier and a few chickens pecked at the ground beside the kitchen. His sword in his hand, Will Scarlet looked about him.

'Where is everyone?' he hissed. 'On a holiday?'

'This way,' Robert said, leading them through an open door.

The three men passed from light into shadow and from the warmth of the sun to the cold of darkness. Now a distant booming reached their ears. It was the sound of cheering – and the clatter of sword against sword. The sound echoed along the corridors, seeming to swell out of the very heart of Clun Castle.

The blood game had begun.

Grendal, the captain of the guard, had come for Nasir shortly before the outlaws attacked the gatehouse. He was armed, helmeted and led into the arena along with the man he must kill. As one, the crowd of wedding-guests rose to their feet, cheering and shouting. Owen lifted a hand.

'Who challenges my champion?' he demanded.

The Marcher lord whose fighter had killed Owen's last champion stood up. He was as tall and as muscular as Owen. They could have been brothers but for the fact that his hair, bound with a leather strap studded with metal, was ginger.

'I challenge him, Owen!' he cried. He gestured at a servant. 'Two hundred marks my man can kill him!'

Owen smiled. Marion stood beside him. She too had smelt the scent of blood and had become intoxicated by it. 'Three hundred he can't!' Owen cried.

The crowd gasped in astonishment. So it was true. Owen had raised the stakes . . . and they had never been higher. The Marcher lord paused. Three hundred marks! It was a king's ransom. But he couldn't back down now. He couldn't lose face in front of his kinsmen. And besides, his fighter was fast, well trained . . .

'Three hundred!' he agreed.

The servant dropped three bags of coins on to the stone floor, three bags that were immediately matched by Gulnar. A signal was given. The crowd roared, and the fight began.

The two gladiators – Nasir and the challenger – wheeled round each other. Like all the fighters before them, they had been robbed of their humanity for the pleasure of the Marcher lords. Their helmets completely covered their faces, the blades curving wickedly out of their foreheads like a single devil's horn. The four swords hovered in mid-air before them, clutched by hands at the end of bare, muscled arms. All around them the onlookers howled and jeered. Marion, standing beside her lord, drank from Owen's cup and looked down into the arena with cruel eyes, her teeth clenched, longing for the climax of the kill.

The blades rang out. The challenger was as strong as Nasir and perhaps a little faster. He had had more experience with the weapons. He had fought – and survived – one blood game already. But Nasir was a born survivor. As the other man rushed him, he parried and blocked.

Just then Robert, Will and Little John arrived.

They remained out of sight, hidden in the shadows on the edge of the arena, watching the two men fight, listening to the cacophony of the crowd. The fight was more furious now, the four swords swinging faster, the sweat shining on the naked arms and torsos of the two gladiators. Robert could hardly believe what he was seeing. It was like something out of the Dark Ages ... or the days of the Roman Empire that his teachers had described to him at Huntingdon Castle.

Will Scarlet was absorbed by the spectacle too. 'I know someone who fights like that,' he muttered, staring at one of the two masked men.

Then Robert froze. Little John followed his eyes upwards.

Marion was leaning towards Owen of Clun, drinking from his cup, her lithe body curled against his. Her face was barely recognizable with the blue paint across her eyes and the loose, wild hair. But it wasn't just her make-up and clothes that made her different. She had become a hell-cat, cheering with the rest of the spectators at the gruesome contest below. It wasn't her, it couldn't be. And yet there could be no mistake. It seemed as if the woman they had come to rescue was already lost.

They were still staring at her when one of the two gladiators died. A subtle move ended the contest. The first fighter – they couldn't tell which was which on account of the masks – had managed to slash the shoulder of the other with one sword. The sight of blood had filled the arena with screams of excitement and pleasure. But then the second fighter had retaliated. He lashed forward with both swords – then charged like a bull. The move caught his opponent unawares. The dagger that protruded from his forehead was perfectly aimed between mask and breastplate. It slid into the other man's throat, slicing through his windpipe and curving upwards into his brain. The man was dead before he knew what had happened.

The shouts of the spectators exploded around the arena. Gulnar shuddered with delight. Grendal smiled coldly. Marion and Owen kissed again. Then the Marcher lord stood up. 'Who challenges my champion?' he roared.

There was a sudden silence. The challenger had just lost three hundred marks. Even now his prize fighter was being loaded on to a cart to be dumped outside the castle walls. Clun's champion was surely unbeatable.

'Come, my lords!' Owen's voice was full of mockery. 'I'll lay ten marks to every one of yours. That's a fair wager.'

Another silence. Ten to one might be handsome odds, but they had seen Owen's champion fight.

Robert tore his eyes away from Marion. She was enchanted – he knew it. Somehow Owen of Clun had made her his slave. She could not be rescued ... at least, not as he had planned. But there was another way.

'Who'll challenge?' Owen demanded, relishing his victory.

Before Little John or Will Scarlet could stop him, Robert had walked out of his hiding-place, out of the shadows and into the light of the arena.

'I will,' he said.

13. THE BLOOD GAME

It seemed to Friar Tuck that he had run ten miles. In fact he had covered only one tenth of that and it had been more of a shuffling trot, but by the time he reached the bonfire he was wheezing like a consumptive horse and his tonsure was gleaming with sweat. But at last he was there. It was absolutely essential that the fire should be lit if Robert's plan were to succeed.

Tuck looked at the bonfire and his heart sank.

The torch had gone out and starting the fire would not be easy, not with the wind shrieking across the moors and the kindling damp after the recent rains. But somehow Tuck had to do it. Once the guards at Clun Castle saw the flames, they would think they were under attack. Robert planned to get away in the confusion.

Hastily, he fumbled in his purse for the two flints he always carried. He drew them out and collected as much dry brushwood as he could find. Then, kneeling down, he struck the two stones together. They sparked but the wind killed any flame before it could be born. Again and again Tuck hammered the stones against each other . . . still without success.

He looked back at the castle, perched on the horizon with the sun just setting behind its crumbling turrets. What was Robert doing right now, he wondered? Whatever it was, he hoped he could do it for a few minutes more.

With a silent curse, Friar Tuck crouched over the brushwood, the flints clattering uselessly against each other in his hands.

Robert pointed his sword at Owen of Clun, his face grim and defiant. 'I accept your challenge!'

Owen stared at him, hardly able to believe his eyes. Of all the people in the world that he might have expected to see that day, the boy from Huntingdon Castle was the last. It was absurd. It was impossible. And yet . . .

'Seize him!' Owen shouted.

Robert made no move to resist as two Marcher soldiers pounced on him. Behind him, in the shadows, Will Scarlet tensed himself to leap forward, but Little John restrained him. The big man didn't yet know what Robert was planning, but already he trusted him enough to let him have his way.

'I'll fight your champion, Owen,' Robert called out, making sure that his words could be heard by every man in the arena. 'But not for money. I fight for your wife!'

And now Owen of Clun realized what had brought Robert to Clun Castle. He should have seen it from the start. The young fool was in love with Marion. He probably had been from the moment he had set eyes on her at the banquet in his father's castle. He had fought for her then; he would die for her now. Owen smiled cruelly and pulled Marion towards him. Marion had ignored Robert. She didn't seem to know who he was . . . nor even that he was there. All her attention was on Owen and once again she urged him to kiss her.

'You're too late, my young fighting cock!' Owen cried, pushing Marion away. 'She's mine.'

Robert turned to the crowd, once again raising his voice. 'Is Owen of Clun fearful he might lose his bride?' he demanded.

It was a clever move. Robert had forced Owen's hand as surely as Owen had forced the hand of the Marcher lord he had challenged before. He did not dare refuse Robert's challenge, not in front of all his kinsmen. Already they were whispering excitedly among themselves. A young stranger, appearing from nowhere; his life for Owen's bride. It was the sort of exploit that the minstrels sang about, the sort of tale they would tell their grandchildren. Owen knew all this and he was furious to be out-manoeuvred on his own wedding-day.

'I accept the challenge!' he thundered, bringing a roar of

approval from the guests. Then he laughed scornfully and leant forward. 'You fool!' he went on. 'Do you really think you can walk into Clun alone and take her from me?'

'Alone?' Robert looked Owen squarely in the eyes. 'I've a thousand men in the valley,' he said.

Owen sank back on to his throne. 'You're too stupid to live,' he sneered. 'My guards would have lit the signal-fire at the first sight of your "thousand men".' He reached out and caressed Marion with the back of his hand. Marion closed her eyes, smiling with pleasure. 'Get him ready!' Owen snapped.

Grendal stepped forward carrying the helmet and breast-plate taken from the dead man and still stained with his blood.

Robert looked at it distastefully. 'I fight as I am.'

Grendal smiled. 'As you wish.'

Robert picked up the two swords that had been set aside for him and moved into the arena. The crowd shouted and cheered at this unexpected treat. Carefully, he examined his surroundings. The arena was circular, hemmed in by a stone wall about six feet high. Above him, on wooden tiers, the audience sat four thick, heads craning over shoulders to get a better view. Robert had once seen a cockfight on a visit to London and the scene reminded him very much of that ... only several times larger.

He looked over his shoulder. Will Scarlet and Little John were still there, pleading with him to be careful – though only with their eyes. It would have been impossible to make themselves heard above the roar of the crowd. He looked back at Owen and Marion, sitting on two thrones on a raised platform perhaps two feet above the rest of the crowd; eight feet above him. There was no way he could reach them, but that was just what he had to do. If he could get to Owen he would have a lever that could get all of them out of Clun Castle.

Finally, he looked at the gladiator – his opponent in the ring. He had watched Owen's champion fight and he had been impressed by the man's skill and speed even if the whole performance had sickened him. He wondered if he could beat him, but deep inside he doubted it. He swallowed, forcing the feeling down. He had to win. There was no other way.

High up on his dais, Owen gave the signal for the blood game to begin. At the same time he leant over to Marion. 'Whatever the outcome,' he whispered in her ear, 'he is a dead man.'

Marion giggled delightedly and leant her head on his shoulder.

Robert had fought Friar Tuck. He had fought Little John and Will Scarlet. Now he fought the last of Robin Hood's men . . . but this time he didn't know it. All he knew, as their swords met, the metal ringing in his ears, was that Owen's champion was deadly. He had no time to plan moves or work out a strategy. He could fight only by instinct, blocking the swirling blades as they sliced towards his throat or stomach, the clamour of the spectators booming all around him.

Little John watched the contest with growing unease. The bonfire should have been lit by now. If Owen thought Robert's army really existed, the fight would come to an abrupt end. The way things were going, the only abrupt end would be Robert's death.

'What's happened to Tuck?' he whispered in Will's ear.

'I don't know!' Scarlet hissed back. 'He could have lit every bonfire in England by now!'

Robert had survived a second murderous exchange. He lunged forward again and the four swords locked, forming a star between the two fighters. Desperately, Robert strained, trying to bring the edges of his blades closer to the champion's neck. His face was only inches away from the other man's mask and as he pushed with all his strength, he saw the razor-sharp edges sliding closer and closer to the bare flesh of his opponent's neck. But at the last minute the champion stepped back. The blades caught the edge of the mask, tearing it off his head.

Nasir stood revealed.

'Nasir!' Robert whispered the word, remembering the face

of the Saracen he had rescued from the hut in Wickham village.

'Nasir!' Little John had seen him too.

'I should have known,' Will Scarlet cried. 'I should have known it was him.'

But Nasir did not know who Robert was. He only knew that the challenger had to die.

Before Robert could utter another word, Nasir rushed him, the swords chopping down from both sides. Robert barely managed to defend himself in time, but in the confusion of slashing metal, one blade nicked the Saracen's cheek, leaving its mark in a streak of blood.

'Kill him!' Owen screamed above the yells of the crowd.

Robert pressed forward, trying to get close enough to Nasir to say a few words without being seen by the crowd. Nasir sprang back, tripped and fell. The guests howled like a pack of dogs. Nasir gritted himself for the kill that must surely come.

But Robert held back and allowed him to get up.

And suddenly Nasir knew that something strange was happening. The young man with the fair hair was looking at him urgently as if he wanted to tell him something. Then his eyes flickered away to the other side of the arena. Still half-expecting a trick, Nasir allowed his gaze to follow them ... and felt a surge of joy and relief as he spotted Little John and Will Scarlet frantically trying to get his attention. Will was shaking his head and pointing at Robert. Little John was smiling. The message was clear. This was a friend. They had come to get him out.

The crowd was beginning to stir, sensing something amiss, so once again Nasir attacked Robert, swinging the swords as furiously as before. But this time he was careful to make sure that none of the blows harmed him. The clash of metal against metal was as loud as ever. The fight looked as savage as before. But now it was all a pretence: Robert and Nasir were fighting on the same side.

Robert allowed Nasir to force him up against one wall. The crowd applauded, thinking that Owen's champion had got the better of him, but in fact it was the only way the two could get close enough to each other to talk.

'Owen,' Robert whispered. 'The platform.'

Nasir understood.

Ignoring the shouts of the spectators, he pulled away from the side of the arena and positioned himself right underneath the platform where Owen of Clun sat. Sensing what was about to happen, Little John and Will Scarlet moved from their hiding-place and began to make their way round the side of the arena. Robert staggered back into the centre of the arena as if exhausted. Nasir was swinging his swords, making intricate patterns in the air. The spectators tensed, waiting for his next move. Then Nasir nodded.

Robert ran forward. Nasir crossed his swords, flat sides up, holding them parallel to the ground. Robert lifted a foot and placed it on top of them. Nasir heaved – and Robert was lifted into the air, high above his head, to land like a cat on the platform beside Owen of Clun. At precisely the same second, Will Scarlet and Little John appeared, their daggers drawn, and before Owen or his wedding-guests knew what had happened, he was in their power, held hostage by no fewer than four pointed blades.

Grendal and six Marcher knights drew their own swords an instant later and raced forward to rescue their lord. But they were too late.

'Drop your swords or I'll kill him!' Robert shouted and pressed the point home by pressing one of his own points into Owen's neck. 'Anyone moves and it's the end of the House of Clun.' He smiled at his prisoner. 'And you wouldn't like that, would you, Owen.'

'I'll see you in hell!' Owen snarled, his face white with anger.

'Make one false move and you'll be there first,' Robert retorted. He glanced at Will Scarlet on the other side of Owen. Will nodded. Little John had grabbed hold of Marion. Nasir was waiting in the arena below.

Carrying Marion with them and forcing Owen down, the three men jumped back into the arena. They had no sooner hit the ground than a steward appeared in a doorway high above.

'The castle's under attack!' he shouted.

Friar Tuck had finally managed to light the bonfire.

'A thousand men!' Robert exclaimed, pulling Owen to his feet. 'And you didn't believe me.'

Either Marion had been knocked out by the fall or she had fainted. Nasir scooped her up in his arms and lifted her over one shoulder. Then, with a quick smile of greeting for his old friends, he followed Robert out of the arena. Owen came with them, still held prisoner between three short blades. Robert had exchanged the clumsy weapons of the blood game for his own dagger.

They went back down the passageways that had brought them in. Behind them, Grendal rallied his men and followed. The crowd was confused. Their master had been stolen away under their very eyes. His champion had joined up with the strangers. And now it seemed that a huge army was on its way to the castle. With the first stirrings of panic, they streamed out of the arena. Nobody knew quite what to do – just as Robert had planned.

Only Gulnar remained behind. The sorcerer was puzzled, for he had not foreseen the events that had just taken place. Oh yes, there would be blood and death. He knew that, he had seen that. But whose? A smile seeped across his lips and his eyes widened. Suddenly he remembered his vision, the evening when he had given Owen the love-potion. A shadow forming a black criss-cross on his master's face. Now, at last, he understood. Blood and death – and what a death! A still-born laugh quivering at the back of his throat, he lurched out to witness the final scenes of the day's drama.

The outlaws were making their way, crab-like, across the courtyard of Clun Castle. Wherever they looked, Marcher soldiers were appearing like black insects out of a grave. They kept Owen between them, their weapons poised at his throat. If Owen got away, they would be slaughtered, cut to pieces in seconds.

A man appeared on a staircase, his spear raised. Robert spun round, firing an arrow. It hit the man in the chest, slamming him against the wall. Little John's knife moved closer still to Owen's throat, cutting the skin. The Marcher lord's eyes, beneath the blue mask, were filled with fear. 'Go back!' he commanded as one of his men tried to sneak up on them. There was the sound of feet crunching on gravel. Owen's head snapped round. 'Stay where you are, you dogs!'

Four men – Robert, Little John, Will Scarlet and, with Marion still unconscious on his shoulder, Nasir. Between them they were holding off an army of more than two hundred as inch by inch, step by step, they drew nearer to the barbican and the portcullis. Overhead, an alarm-bell had begun to sound. The dead body of the guard in the gatehouse had been discovered and outside, as more soldiers had run to spy out the approaching army, Much's arrows had quickly found their mark.

'Back!' Will Scarlet shouted as Grendal and his men tried to cut them off. He and Little John were walking backwards, their daggers clenched beneath Owen's chin. Robert led the way. Between them, the four had become one single creature – forced to look in all directions at the same time if it was to survive. Nasir brought up the rear, his sword waving like a scorpion's tail. 'Back!' he hissed as well. Slowly they continued across the barbican, their hostage trapped between them.

At last they reached the gate. Much was outside, waiting with the two horses. In the distance, the signal-fire that Tuck had lit still blazed.

'Nasir, go!' Robert spat out the command and Nasir obeyed. He still had no idea who Robert was, but there was something about him that reminded him of another leader and another time. Carrying Marion, he ran beneath the portcullis and out on to the drawbridge. Much was so surprised to see the Saracen that he almost loosed off another arrow. Then Little John appeared, looking frantically over his shoulder, waiting for Robert and Will.

At the last possible moment, when it seemed that nothing

could stop them from getting clean away, Owen acted. He was between Robert and Will in the middle of the narrow tunnel that led out of the barbican and beneath the portcullis. On the one side was Much, Nasir, Little John and open country. On the other, the horde of Marcher soldiers was pressing forward, waiting for an opportunity to attack. The tunnel ran for only about twelve feet, divided in two halves by the portcullis . . . but it had become the field for a final battle. If Owen were to stop them it would have to be here.

He moved with all the speed and violence of an angry lion. Will Scarlet was taken completely by surprise: he was thrown back, and the dagger was ripped out of his hand. A second later, Owen was lashing out at Robert's face and neck, swinging Will's dagger with cold, determined hatred. Robert ducked back, his own dagger raised. 'Go, Will!' he shouted. Scarlet hesitated, but only for an instant. He knew what had to be done.

He ran out on to the drawbridge, saw Much and the two horses. 'Now!' he shouted.

'Where's Robert?' Much demanded.

'Just do it!'

Much struggled with the horses, pulling them forward. The ropes that he had tied around their necks snaked across the ground, straightening as they moved. The ends were still fastened to the tree-trunks holding up the portcullis underneath which Robert was fighting for his life. Owen was a man possessed. Twice his dagger had come within an inch of Robert's cheek, so close that he could hear it cutting the air. Much urged the horses on. One of the tree-trunks was pulled away, crashing to the ground behind Owen – but in his fury he barely noticed it. Now the huge weight of the portcullis was supported on only one trunk. Already the top was splintering as the metal teeth bit in.

Owen slashed again, then followed through, pinning Robert against the wall. Robert's weapon was knocked out of his hand. His other hand clasped Owen's wrist, straining to keep the Marcher lord's dagger away from his head. Owen was grinning viciously, confident of his superior strength. At one end of the tunnel, the outlaws were watching, helpless. At the other, the Marcher warriors were waiting to see the young upstart killed. Somehow Gulnar had made his way to their head, his black-swathed body twisting through the crowd.

Out of the corner of his eye, Robert could see the portcullis bearing down on the single tree-trunk. With every second that passed, the wood was cracking and giving way. At any moment the whole thing would come crashing down – and he was right underneath it. And Owen's dagger was inching ever closer to his head, forced towards him with all the Marcher lord's strength.

With a last, desperate effort, Robert pushed Owen away.

The tree-trunk quivered.

Owen was on one side of the portcullis. Robert was on the other.

Then Gulnar screamed. The black criss-cross of his vision was still imprinted on his mad brain. This was the moment he had seen. This moment. 'Now!' he screeched.

Owen heard him and stepped forward towards Robert.

The tree-trunk broke. The portcullis fell.

Owen was right underneath it.

A ton of metal with rusting, pointed teeth thundered into the Marcher lord, hurling him to the ground and almost cutting him in two. For a moment he gazed upwards, death and defeat stark in his eyes. His hand writhed at the dust. Blood cascaded from his mouth.

Trapped behind the portcullis with Grendal and all the other soldiers of Clun Castle, Gulnar raised his hands to the sky, his eyes squirming like maggots in his skull. 'A curse on you, Robert of Sherwood!' he shouted.

But Robert had already gone, running with his outlaws for the safety of the forest.

Owen was dead. The House of Clun was no more.

14. MARION

Marion gazed down at her reflection in the water of a pool: at the blue paint, the jewellery, the straggling hair. 'Is . . . is that me?' She shivered.

'No,' Robert said softly. 'That's how Owen wanted you to be.'

It was the morning after the feast of Arrianrhod. For much of the night the outlaws had travelled, grateful for every mile they could put between themselves and Clun Castle. Robert had reckoned that it would take Grendal and his men at least two hours to raise the portcullis before they could come in pursuit – but either the outlaws had managed to give them the slip or the Marcher lords had forgotten them, staying at the castle to bury their lord. Either way, they were back in Sherwood Forest, alone. The sun was shining.

'They forced me to drink something,' Marion said. 'And then . . . everything was like a dream. A nightmare. Until I woke up.'

But was the enchantment really over or was this another dream? It hardly seemed possible . . . the outlaws together again. 'I am awake, aren't I?' she asked.

'Ay, little flower,' Tuck smiled.

'You're safe,' Much said.

'And Owen's dead,' Will added.

'Dead as skewered mutton,' Little John said.

Nasir nodded.

'You saved me,' Marion said. 'All of you. But . . .'

For a moment she had thought herself transported back a year in time. The outlaws were there, together, just as they had always been: Friar Tuck, red-faced and beaming; Little John in his sheepskin mantle; Much beside him; then Will Scarlet, Nasir and . . .

Not Robin. Robin was dead. Robert.

'Robert of Huntingdon?' she whispered, not yet under-standing. Robert smiled and bowed his head. As Marion turned towards him, she became aware of the heavy torque around her neck. With a sudden grimace, she reached up, tore it off and threw it on the ground in front of her.

Nobody moved. Then Will Scarlet leant down and picked it up, weighing the gold in a practised hand. 'Can't look a gift horse in the mouth,' he muttered. 'Even if it is under a portcullis!'

It was the last day of the month when Sir Richard of Leaford came to Nottingham. A week had passed since Marion had been rescued – though neither the Sheriff nor Abbot Hugo had heard anything of that. They were examining the docu-ment that the Abbot had drawn up, attended by a less than cheerful Sir Guy of Gisburne. Gisburne hadn't been quite the same since his experience in the town of Lichfield. For a start, he was limping, supporting himself on a crutch. And strangely enough, he seemed to have lost his appetite for ale. In fact he hadn't drunk a drop since his return.

The Sheriff, on the other hand, was in a particularly good mood. This was the day when Leaford Grange and all the lands that surrounded it would come into his possession. Naturally he would let his brother have some of it ... after all, it had been Hugo's idea in the first place. He had already spied out a small and rather boggy field behind a hill. He would let the Abbot have that. He might even found another abbey there.

The door opened and Sir Richard was announced. A moment later he appeared, walking in to stand before the two de Rainaults. Neither greeted him with so much as a nod. Standing there in his weather-beaten cloak, he could have been a mere servant as far as they were concerned. Hugo bent his neck over the document. The Sheriff picked at his nails with an ornate paper-knife.

'The last day of the month, Sir Richard,' he said eventually.

'I know.' Sir Richard's voice was hoarse.

'Well, where's the money?' Abbot Hugo demanded.

Sir Richard paused. When he spoke again, his voice was pitiful. 'Hugo!' he cried. 'You're a man of God. I beg you, show me some mercy. Give me another month.'

'And another month after that, I suppose,' the Sheriff cut in.

'You promised it today,' the Abbot added, bleakly.

Both brothers regarded the knight with cold, expressionless faces. In fact they were enjoying the moment immensely. They had been furious when the king had pardoned Marion of Leaford, and they had always detested her father. Now they were seeing him humbled, broken. And the beauty of it was, everything was entirely legal. They could ruin the man, steal his property – and there was nothing anybody could do to stop them.

'You did sign this, didn't you?' Abbot Hugo demanded, holding up the parchment with its four seals. 'You are Sir Richard of Leaford?'

'I was desperate!' Sir Richard pleaded.

'Of course you were,' the Sheriff agreed, hardly able to keep the laughter out of his voice. 'You were desperate to save your daughter. Quite understandable in the circumstances.'

'Unfortunately you failed,' the Abbot continued. 'And now you've failed again, haven't you? Failed to discharge your debts.'

'Most regrettable,' the Sheriff sighed. 'But I'm afraid that, as from today, your lands and Leaford Grange . . .'

'. . . belong to us.' Hugo finished the sentence.

'No mercy, then?' Sir Richard asked.

'None.'

Sir Richard of Leaford looked from one brother to the other. Then, sweeping aside his cloak, he produced two bags of coins and slammed them down on the table. The gold belt, the bracelet and the heavy torque that Marion had been given by Owen of Clun had fetched a good price in Nottingham and Sir Richard had had no difficulty making up the difference.

It had amused him to raise the two brothers' hopes for a while, to make them think they had beaten him, but the amusement had quickly palled. And the knight could stand no more.

'Five hundred gold marks,' he cried.

One of the bags had split open. The Sheriff and the Abbot stared at the glimmer of gold, crestfallen and unbelieving. At the same time, Sir Richard snatched the parchment from Hugo and tore it apart.

'Count it, you conniving villains!' he thundered. 'I'd like to pour every penny piece down your rapacious throats. You cheated me – betrayed me to Lord Owen. Your precious soldiers deserted me.' He turned to face the limping steward. 'Oh yes, you saw to that, didn't you, Gisburne?' Then he paused and smiled to himself. 'Look out of your window, Sheriff!'

In a daze, the Sheriff got up and moved across to the window, his dreams of wealth and property disintegrating. He looked out and shivered with dismay. Marion was out there, Marion of Leaford. She was sitting peacefully on her horse and when she saw the Sheriff she bowed with mock politeness. It was as if nothing had ever happened, as if she had never met Owen of Clun.

'Marion!' he whispered.

'Marion!' Sir Richard said.

Furious, tears of defeat starting in his eyes, the Sheriff backed away from the window and staggered into the room. Then he saw Gisburne, supporting himself painfully against the table, in front of the two bulging bags.

'Well . . . count it, Gisburne!' he half screamed.

He left the room. The door banged shut behind him.

'Will you go back to Huntingdon?'

Sir Richard sat astride his hackney, looking down at Robert. Marion was sitting on a smaller horse behind him. The other outlaws were a short distance away, waiting quietly.

'Not yet,' Robert said.

Sir Richard nodded. There was so much he wanted to say,

so much to be grateful for. But he was a man of few words and, even now, it embarrassed him that his daughter should be associated with outlaws. 'Good fortune attend you,' he muttered and turned his horse away.

Robert and Marion were left together. Sitting there with the sun behind her, her eyes clear again and a gentle smile on her lips, she seemed to Robert to be even more beautiful than ever. She gestured past him to the hill where the outlaws stood.

'Will they accept you as their leader?' she asked.

Robert smiled. 'Would you?'

His answer left Marion unsure what to say. Did he expect her to rejoin the outlaw band? Surely he knew that was impossible. And yet he himself was leaving Huntingdon to stay with them in the forest. Why? For her?

'Good fortune, Robert,' she said, echoing her father's words. 'Herne protect you, my lady.'

Marion reined her horse and rode away.

15. ROBERT OF SHERWOOD

In the weeks that followed, it became painfully clear to anyone who passed through Sherwood that Robin Hood's band was back – and with a vengeance. Every day brought fresh tales of outrage to the ears of the beleaguered Sheriff. It seemed that nobody was safe.

The merchant. He had done very well at Nottingham market. The fine linen cloth that he had bought in London had sold for almost twice the price in Nottingham. As he travelled back through the forest, he was humming to himself, looking forward to a return journey. The tune died on his lips as something whistled through the air and thudded into a tree, inches from his head. His face a sickly white, he turned round and saw an arrow, still quivering in the bark. A moment later, an outlaw – dark-skinned, surely a Saracen – walked up to him and with a jaunty smile cut the bulging money-bag from his belt. There was another of them standing in the bushes, his face hidden by a hood, a second arrow pointed at him. The merchant didn't dare resist. He hardly dared even breathe.

The seneschal. He raised his whip and lashed out again. He was the personal steward of a powerful lord and it was his task to keep the peasants in line, to count every seed of corn and every inch of pasture. Making his rounds of the lord's estate, he had found two peasants asleep when they should have been loading a cart with logs for the manor-house fire. Now he was teaching them a lesson they would never forget. It would be a month before they would sleep again, a week before they could even lie down. The whip arced through the air ... then fell from his hand as an arrow, fired from the undergrowth, buried itself in his neck. The two terrified peasants looked up and just had time to glimpse a hooded figure, disappearing back into the forest. So the rumours were true! Robin Hood was alive. He had escaped from the Sheriff a year ago and at last he had come back to the forest. They glanced at the body of the seneschal, still twitching in the grass. And they smiled.

The forester. He had spotted the trap the night before and had lain in wait for the poacher who must surely come to check it. At last the man arrived, a gaunt, aged fellow dressed in rags, with hollow cheeks and a racking cough. It didn't matter to the forester that the poacher was an honest man, a tanner who had fallen ill and had therefore been unable to work. It didn't matter to him that the poacher desperately needed meat to feed his wife and two children. All that mattered were the rules. The forester was paid to enforce them.

With two burly assistants to help him, he pounced. The poacher, crouched over his rabbit, never even heard them approach. In seconds, the terrified man was firmly held down, one arm extended while the forester drew out his sword. There would be no questions, no trial. The sentence for poaching was well known. He had been caught red-handed; he would depart one-handed.

But before the sword could fall, the forester cried out and lurched forward. The poacher stared. As if by magic, an arrow had sprouted out of the forester's shoulders. At once the two assistants released him and ran for cover, as cowardly as any of the bullies who served the king. The poacher lifted his hand and looked at it, wiggling the fingers. But for the arrow, it would have been severed from his arm. But whose arrow?

A hooded man pushed his way through the bush and stood in front of him.

'Bless you, Robin Hood,' the poacher said.

The man opened his mouth to speak but one of his companions – a huge, bearded man who carried a quarter-staff – glanced sharply at him.

Robin Hood. He was alive again. And he was back.

'It's Robert of Huntingdon,' Gisburne said. 'I know it is.'
The Sheriff sighed impatiently. He was walking outside the

stables of Nottingham Castle, examining his collection of hawks. Ever since he had seen a fine specimen on the wrist of the Earl of Huntingdon, the Sheriff had determined to renew his own interest in the sport. After all, if it was good enough for the nobility, it had to be good enough for him. He had therefore taken to hunting in the afternoon, whenever he was free, and had purchased several birds as well as a falconer to indulge the whim.

'You don't *know*, Gisburne,' he replied. 'You only believe.' He examined a young goshawk, perched on a low fence between two other birds. 'Will he come to the fist?' he asked the falconer. The falconer nodded. The Sheriff turned to Gisburne. 'Believing isn't enough,' he continued.

'It's enough for me,' Gisburne said. 'I'm sure it's him.'

'There's only one way to be sure,' the Sheriff retorted with a sneer. 'And that's to catch him with a longbow in his hand, robbing some wretched traveller. And quite frankly, Gisburne, I doubt if you can manage it.' The Sheriff sniffed with laughter and returned to the goshawk. The goshawk flapped its feathers and shied away from the man – almost as if sensing his malevolence. 'Still seems a bit nervous,' the Sheriff commented.

'My lord . . .' Gisburne tried.

'You're talking about the son – the only son – of one of the most powerful men in England,' the Sheriff reminded him. 'Suppose I did accuse young Robert – and was proved wrong? Can you imagine what the consequences would be? We wouldn't have time to pack our bags!' He clapped his hands and nodded at the falconer. 'I'll hunt with Ajax,' he said. 'And you'd better bring Lancelot as well.'

Gisburne gritted his teeth, exasperated. Despite his misadventures, he was still sure that Robert of Huntingdon and this hooded man, about whom they had recently been hearing so much, were one and the same. The horse he had seen – in Wickham, at Hathersage and in Lichfield – *had* belonged to the Earl's son. He was certain of it. So why wouldn't the Sheriff listen to him?

As if reading his thoughts, the Sheriff smiled. 'I haven't ignored your suspicions, Gisburne,' he said. 'I've sent for a man – Oliver: I think you know him. Tomorrow I'll send him to watch Leaford Grange. We do know where Marion's sympathies lie, don't we? She may try to meet up with the outlaws . . .'

One of the hawks screeched and tore at a piece of raw, bloody meat with a razor-sharp beak. Gisburne glanced at it – at its black, beady eyes and clawed talons. Now it was his turn to smile. The creature reminded him of someone, really it did. But who?

The Sheriff was looking at him suspiciously. Wiping the smile from his face, Gisburne turned and followed his master back into the castle.

That same evening, Robert of Huntingdon – Robert of Sherwood, as he had now become – slipped quietly into Leaford Grange, avoiding the servants who were tidying up in the courtyard and entering through a side door which he had known would be open. Leaford Grange was much smaller than Huntingdon Castle and more like a farmhouse than a castle, despite its tall stone tower. It was arranged in a square, the great hall with its gabled roof running at right angles to the kichen and dairy. A stable and cowhouse completed the square and the whole compound was surrounded by a ditch and a thorny hedge to provide some meagre protection against raiders.

Nobody challenged Robert as he made his way up a staircase beside the great hall to the chamber occupied by Marion. This door was open as well and, after knocking gently, he let himself in. Marion was waiting for him, standing beside her bed. It seemed to her that Robert had grown older in the weeks he had spent in Sherwood Forest. Certainly he was thinner and dirtier than he had been when she had met him at his father's castle.

'Why have you sent for me?' Robert asked in a whisper. One of Marion's servants had been sent into Wickham the day before. Robert had arrived at the village the following afternoon, distributing coins from a recent raid. Edward of Wickham had passed the message on.

'To warn you.' Marion shut the door. 'My steward has a brother who works in Nottingham Castle,' she went on, hurriedly. 'The Sheriff has a plan to unmask you.'

'What plan?' Robert demanded.

'Have you heard of the "king's devil"?' Marion asked.

'Yes.' Had he stayed in Huntingdon Castle, Robert might have remained in blissful ignorance. But outside, in the real world of Sherwood, he had heard the name many times. And it was always spoken with dread. 'He's King John's torturer. The most feared man in England.'

'He's on his way to Nottingham,' Marion said. 'If he reaches Nottingham . . .'

'He won't.' Robert's face was grim.

There was a pause. With just two words, Robert had set Marion's mind at ease. But that wasn't the only reason why she had summoned him to Leaford Grange. 'There's something else . . .' she muttered.

She went over to the bed. There was something lying on the cover, wrapped in a swathe of red cloth. Gently, she unwound it. The object glinted in the light of the oil lamps. A moment later, she held up a sword of brilliant silver.

'Albion!' Robert stared as if afraid to touch it. 'It was his sword,' he said.

'Take it.' Marion held it out towards him.

'No.'

'It's yours,' she insisted. 'By right.'

Robert shook his head. 'Not yet.'

'You're his successor. Herne's son.'

'But I can't accept it.' Robert smiled sadly. 'One day perhaps. When I'm worthy of it.'

'You are,' Marion said.

But still Robert held back and Marion realized that the sword meant more to him than it did even to her. Robin

Hood's sword. Were he to accept it, he would have become Robin Hood. Robert of Huntingdon would exist no more.

She laid it back down on the bed. 'How are my friends?' she asked, breaking the tension that had suddenly come between them.

Robert laughed briefly. 'Glad to be back in Sherwood.'

'Tell them I miss them.'

'Why won't you join us?'

Marion lowered her eyes. 'I can't,' she said. 'My father gave his word when I was pardoned.'

'That pardon was bought . . .' Robert began.

'To save my life.' Marion sighed. 'Do you blame him? I'm his only child.'

'Does he think it will protect you from the Sheriff?' Robert asked.

'I don't know what he thinks,' Marion replied. 'But I know he's afraid that one day I'll return to Sherwood.'

'One day you may be forced too.'

'One day . . .'

Robert was looking at Marion intently. She looked back, but tried to avoid his eyes. There was a long silence, broken by a sudden burst of song from the corner of the room. Marion kept two pet jays on a perch in a cage and one of them had unexpectedly begun to whistle.

'He must be in love,' Robert said.

He reached out and took her hand, then kissed it, his eyes never once leaving her face. Then he slipped out as quietly as he had come in.

The bird in the cage sang on.

16. THE VISION

As soon as Robert had left, Marion went down to the great hall to join her father for a light supper of cold mutton and rye bread, washed down with mead. Sir Richard was in a bad mood. He had just got back from Nottingham, where he had been sent on jury-service, a duty he never particularly enjoyed. As he took off his riding-cloak and slipped on a plain woollen gown, he was scowling.

'What's wrong?' Marion asked.

'It's all over Nottingham,' Sir Richard said. 'They've robbed another merchant and a forester's been killed. It seems that Robin Hood is back.' Marion winced at the name and her father softened. It wasn't Robin Hood. Of course it wasn't Robin Hood. What was he saying? 'Marion,' he muttered. 'I didn't mean . . .'

'I know,' Marion whispered.

'The Earl of Huntingdon's son! Robert of Huntingdon!' Sir Richard's fist crashed down on the table. 'It's incredible.'

Marion looked up nervously. Apart from the outlaws and herself, Sir Richard was the only person in England who knew the secret of the hooded man. 'He saved us both,' she reminded him. 'You can't betray him.'

Sir Richard shook his head. 'I'd never betray him, you know that. But why, Marion? Why is he leading them?'

'Because he was chosen.'

'That's absurd.'

Suddenly Marion was angry. 'You'll never understand, will you?' she said. 'They believe that what they're doing is right, and once I was one of them. I believed it too. I still believe it.'

Her father sighed. This was an argument that they had had

many times before. 'Laws must be changed,' he said, 'not broken.'

'Yes?' Marion countered. 'And how long must we wait to change laws that can blind a man who kills a hare because his children are starving? I've seen those foresters at work!'

Both father and daughter fell silent. Marion's stories of her life with Robin Hood and the outlaws upset Sir Richard as much as Sir Richard's references to Robin upset her. He poured himself some mead, then pushed the goblet away.

'Listen to me,' he said, 'I want you to promise me that you'll have nothing more to do with the outlaws. That part of your life is over. Promise me, I beg you.'

Marion was close to tears. Slowly, she nodded her head.

'There's only one way it can end,' Sir Richard said.

And then she could stay in the room no longer. She got up and ran to the door. For a moment she paused, her hand on the iron ring.

'I lived with that,' she cried. 'I knew that. Every day I was in Sherwood.'

Leaving her father alone at the table, she shut the door and ran back to the solitude of her own room.

The sword Albion was lying on the bed where she had left it. She unwrapped it again and held it in her hands, remembering its history and the history of the man who had owned it. It was one of the seven swords of Wayland, mystical weapons that had been created long before the Normans had come to England. Inside the slender silver blade were trapped awesome powers ... the powers of light and of darkness. It had been entrusted to Robin Hood by Herne the Hunter and in all the time it had been his, he had used only the forces of light, fighting the cruel, the wicked and the wholly evil: the Baron Bêlleme, the Templar Knights, the Brabançon mercenaries, the witch Lillith and, of course, the Sheriff of Nottingham.

Once it had been stolen. Morgwyn of Ravenscar, an abbess whose devotions had turned out to be reserved exclusively for the devil, had taken Albion and had released the darkness within it. Such had been the power of the sword that she had come close to conjuring up Lucifer himself – and would have succeeded had Robin not broken into the Abbey and destroyed the other six swords at the last minute.

Never again must Albion fall into evil hands. At the time of his death, when Robin Hood had known that he must face the greatest enemy and fall before him, he had entrusted Albion to Marion. At the moment that he had given it to her, she had known that she would never see him again and she had wept. But she had guarded it, knowing that, so long as she kept it, part of Robin Hood would never die.

For the hundredth time she examined the blade, wondering why the light, reflected in the metal, seemed so much brighter than the actual light in the room. It was as if Albion were shining with an inner light of its own. She ran her finger along the name, Albion, engraved just below the hilt. Then, turning the sword on its side, she examined the strange symbols that continued virtually down to the point. They were runes, she thought. Perhaps Celtic in origin. But she had no idea what they meant.

Suddenly they seemed to become larger in her vision. Her eyes were fixed on them; they were all she could see. And the light was growing stronger. Marion trembled, wanting to drop the sword, but she seemed unable to. The light was blinding now. The rest of the room vanished. It was as if the sword had slashed through the fabric of the universe and she was tumbling into the abyss. She should have been terrified, but then a voice whispered in her ear, a voice that she knew well – the voice of Herne.

'Herne's son is my master,' it said. 'I cannot slay him.'

Then the light was swept aside like a curtain being drawn back and Marion found herself in a field on the edge of Sherwood Forest. No. She wasn't *in* the field – she was flying above it. There was a cart rumbling along a dirt-track beside a fast-flowing stream. There were two men on it, one bald and ugly, the other a soldier. Even without being told, Marion knew that this was the king's devil, the infamous torturer, on his way to Nottingham Castle. And she knew what was going to happen next.

Much was the first to appear: he ran out of the undergrowth towards the cart and checked the horse. Robert was close behind him, running forward to get a clear aim at the torturer. But then – Marion's heart missed a beat – it all went wrong. The soldier had a concealed crossbow, already loaded. He lifted it and fired. The bolt hit Robert. A moment later Nasir had fired an arrow killing the soldier, while a second arrow, fired by Will, hit the torturer in the chest. But they were too late. Robert had fallen. He lay still.

She reached out to help him, but Albion drew her back. The field seemed to disappear as if down a never-ending tunnel. The light faded. And then she was back in Leaford Grange, in her own chamber, alone.

Marion dropped the sword. It fell to the ground and lay there, the blade dull again.

But Albion had yielded up its secret.

'Herne's son is my master. I cannot slay him.'

17. THE KING'S DEVIL

It had happened just as Marion had seen in her vision.

The bolt had hit Robert in the fleshy part of his leg, narrowly missing the main artery. He had been doubly lucky. Fired at close range, the crossbow bolt could have shattered the bone – and if the shock alone hadn't killed him he would certainly never have walked again. But there had been some distance between him and the cart when the soldier had fired, and his tough leather tunic had afforded some protection. The wound was deep, the bolt still buried in his leg . . . but he was still alive and conscious.

Little John and Will Scarlet were examining the contents of the cart. The king's devil was silent and unmoving, still perched in his seat but now doubled over, the arrow slanting out of his chest. The soldier had been thrown backwards out of the cart and lay spread-eagled on the grass. Little John pulled back a piece of tarpaulin to reveal a grisly collection of instruments. There were pokers to be heated white-hot. There were thumb-screws that would be tightened gradually until they cracked the bone. There were chains, whips, spikes and strange metal objects which you'd need a sick mind to be able to identify.

'Marion was right,' Little John muttered. 'They were tor-turers – on their way to Nottingham. There are branding irons,' he said, pointing, 'manacles . . . terrible things.'

'The cart's full of them,' Will said, his face filled with disgust.

'Throw 'em in the river,' Little John suggested.

Will looked from the torturer to the soldier. 'Them sort of animals deserve to die,' he spat.

He walked across the field to where Robert sat, propped up against a tree with his legs stretched out, the crossbow bolt protruding from his thigh. Robert was doing his best not to show any pain, but he was breathing heavily and his face was white.

'That's coming out,' Will said bluntly, pointing to the bolt.

Robert could only nod. Out of the corner of his eye he could see that Nasir had already lit a fire and was heating his knife in the flames. Friar Tuck was bent over the stream, wetting a cloth to cool his forehead. He watched as the outlaws slowly surrounded him. He gritted his teeth and tensed himself for what was to come. He could only blame himself for what had happened. After all, he had planned the attack and if he had only run a little faster or spotted the crossbow a little earlier . . .

Friar Tuck and Much leant forward and grabbed his shoulders, clamping him down. Nasir approached, the dagger glowing red. Robert closed his eyes and waited.

That evening, the outlaws set up a temporary camp in the forest. They were too far away to make the journey across Sherwood to their usual hunting-grounds, with Robert in a weakened condition. The bolt had come out cleanly and Friar Tuck had managed to staunch the wound before he lost too much blood, but it had still been a terrible ordeal. Robert had managed to sleep a little, but it had been a fitful, shallow sleep, disturbed by nightmares of pain. Now he was awake. His breath was rattling in his throat and he was drenched in sweat – the sure signs of an approaching fever.

'We're taking too many risks,' Little John said.

'It's all risks, ain't it, John?' Will Scarlet muttered, walking back towards Robert. He jerked his head at Nasir who was changing the dressing on the wound. 'I hope he knows what he's doing,' he said.

Nasir looked up from his work. 'The wound is deep,' he said.

'Ay,' Friar Tuck agreed. 'Needs looking after.'

Little John had rejoined the group. 'Who by?' he asked.

Will Scarlet pounded a fist into the palm of his hand. He was furious – furious because there was nothing they could do. 'We don't know nothing!' he hissed.

'Well, the wound'll poison him if it's left like that,' Friar Tuck said.

'What about the old woman?' Much suggested. All heads were turned in his direction. 'The one in Wickham,' he went on. 'She cured my toothache. You should have seen it! She took this little worm and . . .'

'This ain't toothache, Much!' Will interrupted angrily.

Even so, the outlaws had to agree that Much was right. Had Robert been injured while he was at Huntingdon Castle, he would have received nothing but the best treatment. A physician would have been summoned, no matter what the cost. The wound would have been dressed with strong wine and the whites of fresh eggs and he would probably have been bled. But the outlaws could hardly take him to a physician nor even a barber-surgeon now. Too many awkward questions would be raised – and moreover, they actually preferred to put their trust in Meg.

Every village had its Meg, a wise woman (some might say a witch) who knew all the secrets of the local herbs – when to pick them and what spell to mutter while you did. Perhaps she might have a jar of fat, boiled down from the body of a recently executed criminal and purchased – at a price – from the castle hangman. Meg, the wise woman of Wickham, had achieved spectacular results using nothing more than a dead man's tooth. Whatever her methods, though, the outlaws were confident that Robert would be safe in her hands.

Only Will Scarlet grumbled. 'It ain't safe in Wickham.'

'It's not safe anywhere.' Little John beamed at him. 'But as somebody said, it's all risks, ain't it?'

Carrying Robert on a makeshift stretcher, they set off through the forest.

As soon as they had gone, the torturer straightened up. He was a bald-headed man with the body of a wrestler and the hands of a musician. The instruments that those hands played with, Little John had already thrown into the stream.

The king's devil had no friends. What few friends he had once had he had been regrettably forced to torture at one time or another and now there were none left. He did, however, have a great many enemies . . . and this was not the first time that he had been on the receiving end of an arrow. He had therefore taken to wearing a thick jacket cut from leather that had been cured until it was as hard as wood. Even a crossbow bolt fired at close range would have had difficulty penetrating it, and although Nasir's arrow had wounded him, and the blood was still dribbling out of the wound above his heart, he was not dead.

He had sat still throughout Robert's operation, knowing that a single move really would cost him his life. When Little John and Will Scarlet had searched the cart he hadn't even dared breathe. But he had heard everything. And when they had operated on the hooded man, he had slipped open one eye and seen him . . . with the hood thrown back.

Now he got down from the cart, pulled out the arrow and threw it away. He had seen the face of the hooded man and he would not forget it. The Sheriff of Nottingham would pay dearly to know what he knew. That was why he had been called to Nottingham in the first place.

Clutching a hand to the wound to hold back the blood, the king's devil stumbled away from the cart – the outlaws had taken the horse – and set off on foot to find his way to the castle.

'She died a couple of months ago.'

After a journey that had seemed to take them for ever, the outlaws had arrived at Wickham only to be greeted by Edward with the bad news. Meg was dead. She had lived to a grand old age – some said she was well over fifty – but now she was gone.

'Is there anybody else?' Little John asked.

'Not in Wickham.' Edward looked anxiously at Robert.

The journey through the night had not done him a lot of good. His eyes were glassy, the skin stretched tight over his cheek-bones. The wound in his thigh had opened again and his leggings were dark with blood.

'If only Marion was with us,' Much said.

'Well she ain't,' Will Scarlet said.

'Would she come?' Little John asked.

'Ay,' Friar Tuck said. 'She would.'

'Let's ask her.' Much was desperate. 'I'll go now.'

'Wait . . .' The voice, almost too soft to be heard, came from the stretcher. Robert swallowed, trying to get some moisture back into his mouth. 'They could be watching her,' he whispered.

'I can get past anyone,' Much said.

Robert shook his head. 'It's too dangerous.'

'I'll tell you what's dangerous,' Tuck cut in. 'That wound. And the longer you leave it, the more dangerous it's going to get.'

Robert opened his mouth to argue. He didn't want Marion involved. It didn't seem fair to force her out of the relative safety of Leaford Grange. But he was too weak. His head fell back and, as Friar Tuck nodded, Much darted away, sprinting across the stream and into the forest.

'He's right, Robin,' Little John said – then bit his tongue, realizing his error. The other outlaws had heard it too. Nasir's eyes narrowed and Friar Tuck looked away, but for once Will Scarlet was friendly, clapping a hand round the big man's neck. Robin . . . Robert . . . what did it matter now? Robin Hood was dead. And it looked as if Robert might soon be joining him.

18. A BROKEN NECK

Oliver had served the Sheriff for twenty years and had been drunk for ten of them. He was a fat, elderly man with untidy silver hair, blotchy skin and a broken nose. He was drinking from a wineskin now as he crouched behind a wooden cart, keeping watch on Leaford Grange as the Sheriff had commanded. He belched quietly, then lowered the wineskin. At the same moment, a figure flitted across the grounds in front of the Grange and disappeared into the main courtyard. Oliver wiped his lips with the back of his hand. An outlaw? He would have to keep his eyes open.

Having got into the courtyard, Much had to get into the Grange. He looked about him, keeping close to the wall of the stable. He could hear Sir Richard's voice on the other side, giving instructions to a blacksmith. How could he get past him without being seen? There were two servants at work at a wood-pile. As he watched, they hoisted a bundle of logs on to their shoulders and walked through a door at the side of the house. Hastily, Much raised his hood. Then he darted forward, picked up the remaining logs and followed, keeping the bundle between his face and Sir Richard.

The door, divided in two pieces horizontally like a stable door, turned out to be the main service entrance, leading into the screens passage, which would in turn lead into the great hall. Dropping the logs, Much set out to find a staircase that might lead up to Marion's chamber. Instead, all he found was a large and glowering serving-woman who was staring at him as if he had just committed a criminal offence, which, in a way, he had.

'What do you think . . . ?' she began.

'It's all right, Kate,' came a soft voice from behind her. 'I know him.'

Marion stood there, already dressed for a journey, wrapped in a blue travelling-cloak. 'It's Robert, isn't it?' she said. 'He's wounded.'

Much's mouth fell open. 'How did you know?' he demanded.

'Where is he?'

'We took him into Wickham,' Much said. 'But the wise woman's died.'

For a moment the two looked at each other. Marion knew that if she left Leaford Grange now, if she rejoined the outlaws, she might never be able to return. But Robert was hurt . . .

'I'll come,' she said.

Still tied up with the blacksmith, Sir Richard didn't notice Marion as she slipped out of the service door with Much and ran away from Leaford Grange. Oliver, however, did. So the Sheriff had been right once again! Taking a last quick swig from the wineskin, Oliver lurched forward and began to follow.

In Wickham village, the outlaws had almost given up hope. They had moved Robert into the barn, out of the sunlight, but he was burning up anyway. He was awake half the time, asleep half the time – and it worried them that they could barely tell which was which. Nasir was acting as the outlaws' watchman, positioned high up on the thatched roof of the barn. But the horizon was empty. Much had been gone for two hours.

'Any sign of him?' Little John called up.

'Not yet.'

'Maybe she's not coming.'

'She'll come,' Nasir said.

Scarlet walked out into the open and squinted in the sunlight. He found himself surrounded by children who had flocked to the barn once they'd heard that Robin Hood was there. 'Go on, on your way,' he said, waving his hands at them. As one, they ran. Everybody in Wickham knew the stories about Will Scarlet's temper. And every child knew that he was one man you never argued with.

'She should have been here by now,' Little John said.

'Well, she ain't,' Scarlet snapped.

Friar Tuck appeared in the doorway. 'He's still sweating,' he said, shaking his head gravely.

'He's not the only one,' Scarlet muttered.

'It's fever.' It was as if Tuck were pronouncing the death sentence – and indeed, fever killed more men than it spared.

'Well, don't look at me,' Scarlet cried, walking away. 'I can't do nothing, can I!'

Tuck watched him go. 'We've been here too long,' he muttered.

'Ay,' Little John said. 'I know.'

'John!' Nasir called out.

There was a commotion on the other side of the village. Much and Marion had appeared. Edward was with them and there were six or seven villagers behind him. Between them they were carrying what looked like a large sack, dripping wet and obviously heavy. Little John, Friar Tuck and Will ran over to the crowd to see what was happening.

'He broke his neck,' they heard Much cry, plaintively.

The sack was in fact Oliver. It was difficult to say exactly what had happened to him other than that he had somehow managed to get himself killed.

He had followed Marion and Much from Leaford Grange all the way to the edge of Wickham village before they heard him behind them. If they hadn't been so concerned about Robert, they would have heard him earlier, for he was snapping just about every twig and rustling just about every bush he came upon. Much had heard him first and had guessed at once that he must have been watching out for them at the Grange. Signalling to Marion, he had ducked behind a bush, while she concealed herself on the other side of a tree.

Sure enough, a minute later, Oliver had appeared, panting and mopping his brow and wishing that Marion and the outlaw would rest for a while so that he could too. Then, realizing that he could no longer see either of them, he had stopped. He had cocked his ear. There was nothing. Scratching his head, Oliver had forked off to one side, following a path that led down to the bank of the village stream.

He was standing there, balancing rather awkwardly on a log, when Much reappeared. Much had taken out his knife, meaning to challenge Oliver rather than to kill him. But when Oliver saw the muddy, armed and obviously dangerous outlaw pressing through the undergrowth towards him, he had panicked. He had stepped back, lost his footing, slipped and fallen over backwards into the stream. By the time Much had reached him, the man was dead. Too drunk even to fall properly, Oliver had broken his neck.

'He . . . he was following us,' Much was saying now. 'I wasn't going to hurt him. I wasn't going to do anything. He just fell. I never went anywhere near him. He just fell and . . .' With the villagers and the outlaws surrounding him and all eyes on the body, Much's explanation quickly petered out.

'I know him,' Edward said. 'His name's Oliver. He's one of the Sheriff's men.'

Marion gazed down at the body. Then she felt a hand on her shoulder. She looked up. It was Little John. 'Come on, lass,' he said. 'There's nowt you can do for him.' Taking her gently by the arm, he led her away from the crowd and into the barn where Robert was lying.

The villagers, however, remained where they were. They were looking at the body as though it were a poisonous snake and a few eyes were also raised reproachfully at Much.

'What happens now?' Scarlet asked, sensing the change of mood.

Edward stroked his chin. 'If he's found here,' he said, 'we'll be accused of murder.'

'But he fell!' Much insisted.

'Whatever we say, they'll call it murder,' Edward went on. 'That's the law. They'll fine the village. Could be as much as twenty marks.'

This brought a murmur of horror from the villagers. Will

Scarlet understood why. 'Twenty marks!' he repeated. 'That's a fortune. Even if you sold everything you've got ...'

Edward nodded. 'That's why we've got to get him out of Wickham – take him deep into the forest. Is it agreed?'

The villagers muttered among themselves, but there were no two ways about it. If the body were found in Wickham, they would be ruined. It had to go.

'Better wait till nightfall,' Scarlet said.

'No, it's got to be done now.' Edward was not a happy man. 'Bad luck to bury him after dark.'

'Bad luck?' Will Scarlet could hardly believe what he was hearing. 'Who for?' he demanded. 'Him or you?'

But Edward was quite serious. 'Him, of course.'

'He's had his bad luck,' Scarlet said.

'Depends where he's going, doesn't it,' Edward replied. He gestured at two of the villagers. 'Get a cart.'

Scarlet watched in wonderment as the villagers set about their business. He had never understood these country super-stitions. As far as he was concerned, it didn't make any difference if you buried a man in the morning, in the afternoon ... or not at all. He noticed Much standing miserably by himself and tapped him on the arm. 'Cheer up,' he said. 'It ain't your fault. Anyway, he was a spy. Serves him right.'

Together, the two men walked back into the barn. Marion was kneeling beside Robert, seeing to his wound. He was awake now and seemed to be breathing a little more easily, but when Marion straightened up, her eyes were troubled.

'I've done all I can,' she said, adding in a whisper, 'Herne protect him!' She glanced sharply at Little John. 'He mustn't be moved. Not while the fever's on him.'

'How long'll that be?' Scarlet demanded.

'Several days.'

'Days?' Scarlet pushed his way through the outlaws until he was face to face with Marion. 'Look,' he said, 'we've got to get him into Sherwood, build a shelter for him there.'

'We could,' Little John cut in, 'but we're not going to.' He smiled at Marion who looked back at him with gratitude.

'Leave him to us, Marion,' he said. 'We'll nurse him. You get back to Leaford.' He walked over to Scarlet, towering ominously over him. 'All right, Will?'

But Will Scarlet didn't need to be threatened. He could see Marion's distress and he felt it too. 'We'll stay,' he muttered.

Robert groaned. Marion went over to him. 'You shouldn't have come,' he said.

She knelt down and brushed the hair out of his eyes with her hand. 'They're saying you're Robin Hood,' she said in a soft voice.

He nodded. 'In the villages, yes ...'

'And in Nottingham.'

'I never wanted it to happen.'

Marion shook her head. 'It's just a name, isn't it?' she said. 'Robert or Robin ... how can it matter?'

But even so, there were tears in her eyes. Robert lifted a weak hand and brushed one of them away. 'Don't cry,' he whispered.

'No ...' The tears were coming faster now despite herself. Marion tried to smile. 'I'm remembering. I need time. Time ... that's all. I understand. And it's right you should take his name. It's right ...'

She could say no more. Robert's head fell back and his eyes closed. Taking his hand in hers, she squeezed it gently and prayed.

19. THE SHERIFF'S REVENGE

There is a certain technique to falconry. Loose the hawk when the quarry is too close and there will be little or no pleasure in the kill. But if you wait too long and give the bird too far to fly, then you may never see it again.

The Sheriff of Nottingham had a fine hawk. He had one of the most experienced falconers in the country. He had a crowd of grooms and a dozen austringers – foot-servants carrying small frames for the hawk to sit on. He had beaters with spaniels to stir up the game and he had a fast horse on which to pursue it. But he didn't have the technique. He had given his hawk too many long chases and now he had lost it.

'What's happened to the wretched bird?' he demanded. 'Where the devil has it got to?'

Gisburne, riding beside his master, could not keep a malicious smile from his face. 'Flown off, my lord,' he said.

'Rubbish.' The Sheriff dangled a piece of raw meat in his gloved hand. 'It'll come to the lure.'

'You've made it do too much,' Gisburne said in an 'I-told-you-so' tone of voice.

'Don't be absurd,' the Sheriff snapped. 'That peregrine's the finest hawk in the country! It's perched in those trees, gorging itself on ...' He broke off. 'Listen! Can you hear its bells?'

Gisburne listened for a moment. 'No, my lord.'

The Sheriff scowled at him. 'Well, I can hear them.' Pointing to a thick cluster of trees, he spurred his horse forward. Gisburne held back. 'Over there, you deaf idiot!' the Sheriff shouted.

On the other side of the same cluster of trees, Edward of Wickham was watching the hawk as it circled above him, the bell on its leg tinkling softly. There were five villagers with him, two resting by a cart while the other three took their turn digging the hard earth. They had chosen a glade about a mile from Wickham village, a secluded last resting-place for Oliver, who was meanwhile stretched out under a blanket on the cart. Edward watched the hawk but failed to understand its significance. He knew nothing of falconry – except that noblemen frequently rode through his crops while they were about it. The bird had probably escaped from a castle. It meant nothing to him.

He examined the hole that he and his friends had dug. It was about six feet deep and wide enough to accept Oliver's bulky frame. 'That's deep enough,' he said. 'Let's get him off the cart.'

The villagers threw down their tools and turned to the cart. Even with six of them, it was a struggle getting Oliver off. He was even heavier in death than he had been in life and just as uncooperative. They were still struggling with him when the Sheriff burst through the trees, followed by Gisburne and a crowd of grooms, beaters, austringers and soldiers.

'Stay where you are!' Gisburne cried.

The villagers dropped Oliver, who fell clumsily, wedging himself sideways in the grave. They scattered, searching for a way out of the glade, but for once Gisburne had acted quickly. Already he was cutting them off on one side while the soldiers moved in and encircled them. By the time the Sheriff rode up, a smile of curiosity on his face, they were trapped.

'Well, well,' he exclaimed. 'A burial party!'

Gisburne climbed down from his horse and walked over to the grave. 'It's Oliver, my lord,' he said.

The Sheriff's eyebrows rose. This was getting more interesting by the minute. He glanced at the villagers. The man with the ginger beard and the surly, hostile face ... Where had he seen him before? Of course! 'You're Edward of Wickham,' he said.

'My lord,' Edward began, 'g ...'

The Sheriff leant down from his horse. His hand swept

through the air, slamming into the side of Edward's face and almost knocking him to the ground.

'You'll speak when you're spoken to!' he cried.

Edward stood where he was, a bruise already darkening on his cheek.

The Sheriff looked past him into the distance. Everything was beginning to make sense to him. 'Wickham . . .' he muttered.

In Wickham, Robert's condition had changed for the worse. He was still trapped in the nightmare land between sleep and consciousness – and when he was awake, he seemed only half-aware of where he was. But worse still, his wound had become infected. It looked as if he must surely lose the whole leg. Marion had said that he should remain in the village for several days. She had been optimistic. The way things were going, he would be lucky if he ever left.

Nasir was still perched on the roof of the barn, keeping watch. It was Nasir who now saw the Sheriff approaching the village with Edward and the other villagers in chains behind him.

'The Sheriff and Gisburne!' he shouted, sliding down on a rope. 'They've got Edward!'

Inside the barn, Scarlet spun round, his eyes blazing. 'Now we've *got* to move him!' He ran forward and grabbed one end of the rough wooden bed on which Robert was lying asleep. 'Tuck! Much!' he commanded.

A moment later, with Scarlet and Little John at the front, the four outlaws were racing out of the barn carrying Robert between them. As the Sheriff approached from one side, they were joined by Marion and Nasir and fled out of the other, splashing through the stream and clambering up the slope that led them into the shelter of the forest. They were only just in time. No sooner had they set the bed down and flung themselves behind the bushes than the Sheriff had arrived.

'Search the village!' he called out.

At once his soldiers sprang into action, brutally pushing the villagers aside and causing as much damage as they could while they turned the cottages and houses inside out.

'That was close,' Scarlet panted.

'I reckon they were looking for you, little flower,' Tuck said.

'They've no proof,' Marion muttered.

Scarlet was looking back at the village. 'They won't get much out of Edward,' he said.

'No.' Tuck smiled. 'And nothing out of Oliver!'

'Marion . . . Marion . . .'

Tuck's smile quickly faded as Robert's tortured voice reached him from the bed. The brief, hurried journey had worsened an already critical condition. Robert was burning up with fever, his hair damp with sweat. For the first time, Tuck became aware of how acute the danger really was. It seemed that the outlaws had found Robert only to lose him again.

'He will come through it . . . ?' Little John asked.

'He will,' Marion said, her voice no more than a whisper.

'But you're not sure, are you?' Little John said.

'I can't be.'

In Wickham village, the Sheriff finished his search. There was no sign of the outlaws, but he was not disappointed. Things had worked out rather well. For weeks he had been smarting at the humiliation he had received at Sir Richard's hands. His house – Leaford Grange – and all the lands around it should have been his! But now, sooner than expected, he would have his revenge.

Crouching not a hundred yards away, the outlaws watched him go. They were about to return to the village when there was a rustling behind them and an old man appeared and walked towards them, carrying a staff. He had come out of nowhere, but Will Scarlet recognized him at once – the long hair, the solemn, ageless face.

'Herne!' he whispered.

The spirit of the forest had come to them in human form. He had come to tend to his son.

'Herne . . .' Little John began.

'Leave me with him,' Herne commanded. 'Take Marion back.'

Slowly, reluctantly, the outlaws moved away. Herne looked down at Robert sadly. His son was close to death, but Herne had come to pull him back into the land of the living. Gently, he placed an outspread hand on Robert's forehead, the fingers forming a star. As the power of Herne flowed into him, Robert opened his eyes and smiled, the pain far away.

'Your enemies are about to take Albion,' Herne muttered.

'Albion?'

'Before long you will learn its mystery. Sleep now!'

Robert closed his eyes again and slept. The healing had begun.

As Herne had commanded, the outlaws escorted Marion as far as Leaford Grange, leaving her in front of the courtyard. They were sad to see her go. Despite the circumstances, they had been glad to see her that day. They had been together again, as in days past. But nobody tried to talk her into staying with them. They knew that she would have to make that decision for herself.

Still wearing her travelling-cloak, Marion hurried back into the house and through the screens to the great hall. The first person she saw when she got there was her father. He was sitting in a chair, his face ashen-white.

'We were beginning to wonder where you were,' a familiar voice rang out. 'Weren't we, Sir Richard?'

Marion twisted round. The Sheriff of Nottingham was sitting in her father's chair at the high table, his face flushed with vicious pleasure. Gisburne and four soldiers stood around him. But worse than all this was the object that the Sheriff held, resting it on his lap.

He had searched her room. He had Albion.

'Gisburne suggested you might have been captured by outlaws,' the Sheriff went on in the same oily, sarcastic tone. 'But I thought that highly unlikely.'

'My lord Sheriff,' Marion began, 'I ...'

'No!' The Sheriff smiled icily. 'I'd rather you didn't tell me now. Not now. It would spoil the surprise, wouldn't it? Of course, I'm dying to know . . .' His eyes darkened. '. . . but I'd prefer to wait until we're back in Nottingham.'

Marion stared in horror. Sir Richard sprang to his feet. When the Sheriff had arrived and Albion had been found, he had felt nothing but shame and disappointment. Marion had broken her vow to him. Despite what she had promised, she had seen the outlaws once again. But this . . .

'This is monstrous!' he rasped. 'You can't take her to Nottingham!'

The Sheriff was enjoying himself enormously. 'I can do what I please,' he said.

'She's done nothing!' Sir Richard protested.

'We'll see, won't we?'

The Sheriff flicked a hand in Marion's direction. Gisburne and the four soldiers moved forward. Sir Richard could only watch as they dragged her out of the great hall.

Marion was a prisoner. Once again Sir Richard was alone.

20. PRISONERS

Early the next morning, a horseman left Leaford Grange and set off at a gallop into Sherwood Forest. Sir Richard might not be able to forgive Marion for what she had done, but he couldn't abandon her to her fate either. There was only one man in the country who could help her now ... as he had helped her before. And Sir Richard intended to find him.

Crusades, politics and too many betrayals had hardened Sir Richard. His wife had died young, leaving him with a headstrong and unmanageable daughter. Although he loved her in his own way, he had never been able to understand her. Rather than enjoying the peace and security of Leaford Grange, she had deliberately chosen the dangers of life in Sherwood Forest ... and not once, but twice! King John himself had pardoned her. How could she have put that pardon at risk by returning to Wickham?

As Sir Richard rode on, he was unaware that he was being watched. Much was perched in a tree, high above the road, and seeing the knight approach he swung down on a rope and rejoined the other outlaws.

'Sir Richard, I reckon,' he said. 'Coming this way.'

'Is he alone?' Scarlet asked.

Much nodded.

'Something's wrong,' Little John muttered.

A minute later Sir Richard had reached them. Seeing the outlaws, he reined in his horse, looking down at them angrily. It was as if they were to blame for everything that had happened to his daughter.

'Where's Robert of Huntingdon?' he demanded.

'There ain't no Robert of Huntingdon in Sherwood,' Scarlet replied.

'He's Robin Hood,' Little John added.

Sir Richard sighed here, exasperated. He was in no mood to play games. 'Where is he, Tuck?' he asked.

But Friar Tuck's answer only infuriated him all the more. 'He's with Herne.'

'Don't fool with me,' Sir Richard snapped. 'Marion's being held by the Sheriff.'

This was the last thing the outlaws had expected and abruptly their mood changed. Sir Richard had never really been a friend to them. But if his daughter was in danger, they would do anything to help.

'Robert was wounded . . .' Little John said.

'So you went for her!' Sir Richard cut in, his temper rising. 'You put her in danger.'

'She came willingly.'

'Where is he now?' Sir Richard asked.

'I've told you,' Tuck muttered.

'With Herne!' Sir Richard's voice was full of scorn. 'I haven't time for superstitious nonsense. My daughter's life is in danger.'

Scarlet shuffled forward to Little John, his fists clenched. 'I knew this would happen,' he said.

Suddenly the two men were at each other's throats.

'You agreed to it.'

'You did, not me!'

'Then why didn't you say so?'

'Because you never listen!'

It almost looked as if a fight were going to develop. Then Much sprang between them. 'Stop it!' he cried. He waited until Scarlet and Little John had calmed down. 'Quarrelling won't help Marion, will it?'

Little John sighed. It had been just like this after the death of Robin Hood. For some reason, without a leader the outlaws just couldn't get on together. Robin hadn't just led them, he had united them. And in a strange way, Robert had been doing just the same.

'We don't know where he is,' he said, tiredly.

'I'm here.'

The outlaws spun round. Robert had been standing on a hillock at the edge of the track, but now he walked down towards them. He was limping, but the fever was gone. His old colour had returned and his eyes were bright. Not for the first time, they marvelled at the powers of Herne . . . the powers of light and darkness that made all things possible.

Robert nodded at Sir Richard. He had overheard the entire conversation and already he had a plan. 'I'm going to Nottingham,' he told them.

'You're crazy,' Scarlet said.

Robert smiled. 'They may suspect me, but they've still no proof. I'm Robert of Huntingdon, remember? The son of the Earl.'

'How can that save Marion?' Little John asked.

'The Newark road,' Robert muttered, speaking almost to himself.

'The Newark road?' Much repeated.

'What are you talking about?' Tuck asked.

Robert drew closer to his friends. For the moment, Sir Richard was forgotten. 'Listen . . .' he began.

Meanwhile, in the great hall of Nottingham Castle, the Sheriff was enjoying a late breakfast, cutting up a joint of cold beef with a gleaming dagger. He was in a glorious mood. It seemed at last that everything was going his way. Edward and the other villagers were his prisoners. So was that accursed Marion of Leaford. The torturer – the king's devil – was expected any day now. And his servants had even managed to find Ajax, the lost falcon. As Gisburne watched, he pronged a piece of meat on the point of his dagger and held it out to the hawk. Ajax tore at it greedily, its black eyes winking beadily at its master.

'There's a good boy, Ajax,' the Sheriff murmured. He turned to his steward. 'You know, Gisburne, if he hadn't flown off, we'd never have found out about Oliver, would we?' he cried. He chose another piece of meat and offered it to his pet. 'Who's my precious, eh?' he warbled. 'Who's my beauty?'

Sitting at the table next to the Sheriff, Gisburne's eyes were drawn to Albion which lay among the scattered remnants of the meal. Gisburne, who considered himself the equal of any swordsman in Nottingham, had never seen quite such a fine weapon. Albion. He had read the name beneath the hilt but had ignored the runes that ran beneath it. What Gisburne didn't understand, Gisburne didn't want to know. He weighed the sword in the palm of his hand. It was beautifully balanced, a real craftsman's weapon. Perhaps the Sheriff might even consider . . .

The next moment, the Sheriff lashed out with the flat of his dagger, knocking Albion out of his steward's hand. He had seen the greedy look on Gisburne's face. But Albion was his!

'Get the girl,' he commanded.

Giving the Sheriff a look of pure poison, Gisburne got up and left the room. The Sheriff waved another piece of meat under the hawk's beak, but the bird had eaten its fill. Still clutching the dagger, he stood up and ambled down to the end of the great hall where Edward and the villagers were waiting, chained together and squatting against the wall. Again the Sheriff held out the dagger – this time under Edward's nose. To him, the prisoners were no more than animals. Even the hawk was more valuable than them.

'Not hungry are you?' the Sheriff sneered. With a quick movement he flicked the scrap of meat off the end of the dagger, then held the blade flat against Edward's cheek. 'I'm going to hang you,' he snarled. 'I should have done it a long time ago. You murdered my man Oliver in your village, didn't you?'

'What reason would I have to kill him?' Edward replied.

'Because he'd followed the Lady Marion there, hadn't he?'

But Edward wasn't going to let the Sheriff draw him into giving anything away. 'Had he, my lord?' he said.

The Sheriff laughed softly. 'You know, Edward,' he said, 'the king is sending me two very experienced interrogators. I promise that you shall be the first to test their instruments.'

There was a movement at the other end of the hall and

Gisburne came back in, escorting Marion. 'The Lady Wolfs-head,' he announced, repeating the same, cruel gibe that he had used at the banquet in Huntingdon Castle.

'Good morning, Lady Marion,' the Sheriff said, straightening up and walking languidly towards her. 'I trust you slept well.'

Marion regarded him as though she were his mistress rather than his prisoner. 'My lord Sheriff,' she said, haughtily, 'I wish you to tell me why I'm being held in Nottingham.'

The Sheriff smiled to himself and picked up Albion. Marion's eyes flicked towards the blade but her face gave nothing away. 'Albion,' he said, as if that were answer enough. 'You want revenge. You went to Wickham to meet up with your fellow outlaws. Oliver followed you there and at your instigation he was murdered.'

'No!' Marion cried.

'Then tell me what did happen.' The Sheriff gestured at Edward and the villagers with the point of the sword. 'Otherwise, these men will die.'

But Marion said nothing. The Sheriff's eyes narrowed. Why wasn't she afraid of him? Why wasn't she talking? 'Get them out of here!' he commanded.

With a great rattling of chains, Edward and the other villagers were led out of the hall. The Sheriff sat down again, resting Albion on the table. 'Of course, there is a way you can save them – and yourself,' he said. He stretched out a finger and thumb and plucked a grape from the fruit bowl. He was still watching Marion like a hawk . . . as, indeed, was the hawk. 'Just tell me the name of the outlaws' new leader,' he said.

'His name?' Marion repeated.

'Yes . . . ?' This was the moment the Sheriff had been waiting for.

'His name is Robin Hood,' Marion said.

Shaking with rage, the Sheriff got to his feet. Behind him, the hawk pounded the air with its feathers and screeched. Slowly, he approached Marion, his eyes bulging, his mouth stretched in a rictus of hatred. There was a window shaped like a cross behind him and the light was streaming in over his shoulder, illuminating one half of his face while the other was cast into black shadow.

'You devious drab!' he shouted. 'Do you think you can make a fool of me, Robert de Rainault, the High Sheriff of this county, responsible for law and order, appointed by the king? *Tell me his name!*'

'Never!' Marion whispered.

The Sheriff was in a frenzy, his voice quivering on the edge of insanity. 'Then you will never, never leave Nottingham!'

He paused, panting heavily. Behind him there was a heavy footfall on the paved floor of the great hall as somebody limped towards him. He turned round and gaped.

There was a young man standing in front of him, richly dressed in the fine robes of a nobleman. He was smiling apologetically.

It was Robert of Huntingdon.

21. A GREAT FRIENDSHIP

Robert de Rainault regarded Robert of Huntingdon with a look of total astonishment. Beside him, Gisburne could only gape open-mouthed. Sir Guy was still absolutely certain that the Earl's son had, for some reason or other, assumed the mantle of the hooded man. Neither of them had seen Robert since the banquet at Huntingdon Castle and the fight with Owen of Clun. That he should simply walk – or limp – in now was the last thing they could have expected.

Marion was even more astonished than the Sheriff. The last time *she* had seen Robert, he had been close to death, stretched out on a makeshift bed outside Wickham village. Somehow he had made a miraculous recovery. But what was he doing here?

'Sheriff,' Robert said, limping forward, 'I felt it only right that I came directly to Nottingham and told you everything.' The Sheriff glanced at Gisburne, hardly able to believe what he was hearing. Was Robert of Huntingdon about to admit that he was indeed Robin Hood? 'I find it difficult to confess ...' Robert went on.

'Take all the time you need,' the Sheriff said, encouraging him.

Robert sat down heavily in a chair and stretched out his wounded leg. For a moment he paused. All eyes were on him.

'I've been attacked by Robin Hood!' he said at last.

There was a stupefied silence.

'What?' the Sheriff whimpered.

Robert leaned forward, his face creased up with shame. 'Believe me when I tell you that I fought hard and long before they overwhelmed me,' he said. Now that he had started there was no stopping him. 'But the disgrace of being beaten by such scum is something I find almost impossible to bear. Imagine it, Sir Guy. A trained swordsman being beaten by peasants! I doubt if my father will ever forgive me.'

There was a second, long silence. The story – if it was just a story – had been told with remarkable conviction and it did make some sort of sense. After all, the young nobleman was limping. And why else should he have come to Nottingham Castle?

'You were wounded?' Gisburne asked.

Robert nodded. 'An arrow.'

'We'll have it looked at,' the Sheriff said.

'Thank you, my lord.'

Ignoring Marion now, the Sheriff moved closer to Robert. 'This villain who's calling himself Robin Hood,' he said. 'Could you describe him?'

Robert considered. 'About my height,' he said. 'And fair-haired too.'

The Sheriff glanced at Gisburne. 'Could he be mistaken for you?' he asked Robert.

Robert looked up indignantly. 'Certainly not!' he declared. 'He was a peasant!'

'Of course,' the Sheriff chuckled.

Robert seemed to notice Marion for the first time. He stood up with difficulty and moved towards her. 'How is your father, my lady?' he asked. His back was to the Sheriff now and he winked quickly.

'He's well,' Marion said.

'And what brings you to Nottingham?'

'I brought her here,' the Sheriff said. 'Lady Marion's past had been catching her up ... almost tripping her up, one might say. To be blunt, she's been meeting old friends. I hardly need tell you who they are.'

Robert raised his hands in mock amazement – but only Marion could tell that he was play-acting. 'You believe him?' she asked.

'Why should the Sheriff lie?' Robert replied. 'Why would he treat you unjustly?'

'One of my men is dead, Robert,' the Sheriff said. 'She had him killed. And furthermore, she knows the name of her dead husband's successor.'

Robert turned back to Marion. 'Is this true?' he demanded. 'You know the man?' Marion said nothing, so he went on. 'Marion,' he pleaded, 'tell the Sheriff. Tell him who it is. It's your only chance.'

But still Marion refused to speak.

'You see?' the Sheriff cried. 'As stubborn as a mule!'

Robert gave Marion a long, hard look. Then he limped over to the Sheriff, putting his arm confidentially round the older man's shoulders. 'Put her in the dungeons,' he muttered. 'That should bring her to her senses. And loosen her tongue.'

It had not even occurred to the Sheriff to put the daughter of a country knight into the common dungeon. Now he looked at Robert with renewed interest. Perhaps he had misjudged the boy on their first meeting. He seemed to be sullen, cruel, vindictive and completely without pity. In other words he was a young man very much after his heart!

'I've misjudged you, Robert,' he said. 'You may as well know that Gisburne here ...' Gisburne paused, a goblet of wine half-way to his lips. '... had the absurd idea that *you* had become Robin Hood.'

Robert gazed at the Sheriff, his whole body quivering with outrage.

The Sheriff laughed. 'Take her to the dungeon,' he snapped. Gisburne got up and led Marion away. 'I insist you stay in Nottingham until you're quite recovered,' he said to Robert.

Robert smiled. There was nothing he would like more.

They took lunch together that afternoon, Robert and the Sheriff, and as the food was served and the wine flowed, it seemed that the greatest of friendships had been struck. The young man was not only an excellent connection – he was, after all, the son of an earl – he also shared the same sense of humour as the Sheriff, not to mention the same cruel streak.

'Here's another for you, my lord,' he said as he poured the

Sheriff yet another goblet of wine. 'How does a forester shake a poacher's hand?'

'I don't know,' the Sheriff burbled. He was more than slightly tipsy.

Robert dangled his own hand in front of the Sheriff's face. 'On a piece of string!'

The two howled with laughter while Gisburne looked on, confused. It seemed impossible and yet he had been so sure about Robert of Huntingdon. How could he have been mistaken? The fight with Owen, the grey horse, the rescue of Marion . . . it had all added up. But somewhere he had made a false calculation.

'And now, my lord, to a more serious matter,' Robert said. 'The capture of this man who calls himself Robin Hood.'

'Not now, Robert.' The Sheriff waved a hand petulantly. 'It's late.'

'My lord,' Robert insisted, 'I've been robbed and humiliated. I won't rest until he's brought to justice!'

'My dear Robert . . .' The Sheriff hiccuped. 'With the best will in the world . . .'

'Hear me out, my lord,' Robert interrupted. 'I have a plan.'

'A plan?' Gisburne glanced angrily at him from the other side of the table. 'Do you think there's a plan that hasn't been tried?'

Robert smiled amiably at him. 'Forgive me, Guy,' he said. 'I've no wish to decry your efforts, but I believe I have the answer.' He leant forward. 'Listen. It would be impossible for the villains to get into the castle and free the prisoners.'

'I would hope so,' the Sheriff muttered.

'Right. And so we make it easy for them!'

'Easy?'

Robert nodded. 'We use your prisoners as bait. Worms on a fishing-line.' He looked from the Sheriff to Gisburne. 'Let it be known that they are to be taken under guard to . . . say . . . Newark,' he explained, acting as if he had chosen the first name that had come into his head. 'Yes, Newark. You can say it's for further questioning. The Newark road is wooded on either side. So you put the prisoners in a cart. Then you, Guy, myself and as many soldiers as we can muster follow the cart, keeping hidden in the wood. We also send a couple of foresters ahead to warn us if the outlaws are there.' His lips spread into a slow smile. 'We don't do anything until they make their move,' he went on, 'but when they attack the cart, we attack them. And we'll have the whole lot of them in the bag before nightfall.'

He paused dramatically, his hands raised. 'There you are, Sheriff,' he said. His eyes challenged him to disagree. 'It can't go wrong.'

But the plan did go wrong, horribly wrong. For how was the Sheriff to know that before Robert had gone to Nottingham Castle, he had told the outlaws exactly where to be and when?

The cart carrying Edward and the villagers left the castle the following morning with only four guards on either side. That was the bait. The Sheriff, Gisburne and Robert rode close by, keeping out of sight behind the trees. Another twenty soldiers brought up the rear, and two foresters went ahead, to warn the Sheriff as soon as the outlaws were sighted.

The foresters were the first to go. Neither of them knew what hit them – though in fact it was a pair of quarter-staffs wielded by Much and Little John. Their part in the affair was over in seconds. Two blows and they were unconscious. Nobody had heard anything. Nobody knew anything was amiss.

Gisburne and the Sheriff were next. Their path took them beneath a cutting where the side of a hill rose up steeply beside them. With no advance warning from the foresters, how were they to know that Will Scarlet and Nasir were crouching on the top, waiting for them? As they rode past, the two outlaws leapt. They plummeted out of the sky like mythical, flying creatures. Gisburne and the Sheriff just had time to glimpse two black shapes looming out of the sun. Then they were thrown to the ground and knocked unconscious.

What followed was total confusion.

The soldiers scattered, half a dozen of them falling as arrows hit them from nowhere. For nobody could see the attackers. They were being attacked by an invisible enemy, lost in the green haze of the forest. The cart with the prisoners ground to a halt. Nobody was quite sure what was going to happen next – or to whom.

Gisburne groaned and opened his eyes. The Sheriff was crouching next to him, shaking his head, his helmet knocked askew. He turned round to see if Robert was all right. But Robert was gone.

'Move and you die!' Little John's voice echoed out of the forest.

'They've got Robert!' Gisburne hissed.

'What?' The Sheriff's face fell. He almost wanted to burst into tears. Only yesterday everything had been going so perfectly – and now this! It was unfair. Why was his life always such a mess?

'Sheriff!' Little John called out. 'Get on your feet. We have the Earl's son. What's he worth to you, Sheriff?' There was a pause. The soldiers were peering frantically at the undergrowth, swinging their crossbows from left to right. But it was all in vain. There was nobody for them to aim at. 'I'll tell you, shall I?' Little John continued. 'The Lady Marion, Edward and the others.'

'You filthy villains!' the Sheriff raged.

'Don't call us names, Sheriff,' Little John shouted. 'Send Gisburne to get them.'

Crouching in the undergrowth, Robert was watching the scene with amusement. It had all worked out just as he had hoped. In another few minutes, Marion, Edward and the villagers would all be free – and the Sheriff would never even know how he had been tricked.

'What happens when he brings 'em?' Will Scarlet asked, squatting beside him.

'You release me,' Robert said.

'You're going back?' Scarlet shook his head. 'Why?'

'So they won't suspect us, Will.' Robert grinned. 'Robert of Huntingdon is proving very useful to us!'

But 'Robert of Huntingdon' had been far from useful to the Sheriff.

'Fetch them, Gisburne!' he snarled, his eyes swollen with anger. Why had he ever listened to that idiot boy? If it hadn't been for Robert of Huntingdon, he would still have Marion, Edward and the others securely locked up in Nottingham Castle. Another few days and he could have hanged the lot of them. But the Earl of Huntingdon would skin him alive if Robert were killed by the outlaws.

'My lord . . .' Gisburne began.

'Fetch them!' the Sheriff thundered.

He would have to release his prisoners. He simply had no choice.

22. THE POWER OF ALBION

'So much for your splendid plan to catch the villains!'

Robert was sitting gloomily in the great hall of Nottingham Castle while Sir Guy of Gisburne berated him. Even more gloomy was the Sheriff, who sat beside him. It was incredible. He had had them in his hands! And he had lost them!

'Because of you, Marion is free,' Gisburne went on. 'Edward's free. They're all free.' He turned on the Sheriff. 'Why did you listen to him?' he cried. 'Just because he's an earl's son ...'

'Be silent!' The Sheriff's fist crashed down on the arm of his chair. It was fine for Gisburne to insult Robert, but he drew the line at being insulted himself.

'Sir Guy is right,' Robert said, nodding his head sadly. 'But for me you'd still have Marion.' He buried his face in his hands. 'To be held hostage!' He was silent for a moment, then, suddenly determined, he looked up. 'I shall stay here in Nottingham,' he declared. 'Together, we'll seek another way to bring about the downfall of this wolfshead.'

The Sheriff stood up hurriedly. 'Er ... no, Robert, no!' He swallowed. Twenty-four hours of this young man's company had already been quite catastrophic enough. 'You must return to Huntingdon, to your father. And,' he smiled weakly, 'in future, I beg you, keep well away from Sherwood.'

Meanwhile, a servant had entered and had whispered a few words in Gisburne's ear. Gisburne frowned and stood up, disappearing into the shadows at the far end of the hall.

'You're lucky to be alive,' the Sheriff went on as he escorted Robert towards the door. In fact he meant that *he* was lucky that Robert was alive.

'I owe it to you, Sheriff,' Robert said. 'And I know my father will show his gratitude.'

That at least brought a smile to the Sheriff's face. 'No need for anything like that, my dear Robert,' he muttered, wondering how large a gift the Earl might send him for his services.

Gisburne was standing in the doorway, talking to a bald, ugly man with a gaping wound in his chest and a tunic that was thick with dried blood.

The king's devil.

Weak and hungry, it had taken him three days to cross the countryside on foot and reach the castle. But now at last he had arrived. And he had a story to tell.

'You shot Robin Hood?' Gisburne was asking.

'In the left leg, my lord,' the torturer said. 'Above the knee.'

Gisburne glanced over his shoulder. Robert was limping slowly towards him, talking to the Sheriff. His wound was in his left leg.

'Is that the man?' Gisburne asked.

The torturer squinted. He was close to death, although he didn't know it. Too much of his blood had been sprinkled on the leafy ground of Sherwood. But while he lived he could still do harm. 'That's him!' he said.

'A safe journey, Robert,' the Sheriff said.

'Thank you, my lord,' Robert replied.

'My homage to the Earl.'

'I'll tell him,' Robert added.

Gisburne drew his sword.

Robert and the Sheriff froze.

'Gisburne!' the Sheriff hissed.

'I was right from the start,' Gisburne cried, ignoring him. 'Wasn't I ... Robin Hood?'

'Have you gone mad?' the Sheriff demanded.

'This man is the torturer, my lord.' Gisburne pointed at the king's devil who was leaning against a wall, barely able to stand. 'He's the man you've been expecting. He was ambushed by "Robin Hood". *But not before he'd shot him in the leg!*'

Robert looked past Gisburne at the bald, sweating man. It was a face he remembered well. At the same time, the Sheriff was looking at him with rapidly growing suspicion. For perhaps half a second Robert considered bluffing it out. But Gisburne was already approaching him. It was too late.

He reached out, grabbed hold of the Sheriff and pushed him into Gisburne. At the same time, he drew his own sword. The servants scattered. With a thrill of pleasure, Gisburne shoved his master out of the way and pressed forward. He had been right all along. And this was where he would finish it.

Their blades engaged and in the first exchange Robert realized that Gisburne was his equal as a swordsman. More than his equal – for he was still weak from his wound. After parrying off a dozen lethal blows he was forced to support himself against a chair to rest. But Gisburne hadn't even begun. He sliced downwards again. Robert leapt back. The corner of the chair exploded in a shower of wood chippings as Gisburne's sword bit through it.

Now they fought across the tables. Only twenty-four hours before, the Sheriff and Robert had sat there, eating and drinking together, telling jokes. Now the flat wooden surfaces were a barrier between the two fighters while their blades clashed again and again above them. And what of the Sheriff? As soon as Robert had his back to him, he drew his own sword, meaning to finish the fight in the most cowardly way possible. But at the last moment, Robert heard him creeping up behind. He turned, lashed out and wounded the Sheriff in the side. With a wheezing gasp the Sheriff crumpled, falling to the ground in a puddle of his own blood.

Gisburne lunged forward, going for the kill, but Robert had been expecting the move. His sword swept down, crashing into Gisburne's weapon just below the hilt. Gisburne's fingers were momentarily numbed. He dropped the sword. He was unarmed.

But only for a few seconds. There was another sword, lying on the table where it had been left the night before. Gisburne had already admired its fine balance and workmanship. Now he was able to put it to the test.

Albion.

He scooped it up and stabbed at Robert, driving him back into a corner. Robert was badly positioned, hemmed in. He needed more room to manoeuvre and he got it. One slash of his sword cut through a rope holding up an iron chandelier. Then, using the rope, he swung himself across the table and into the centre of the hall. He let go of the rope and the chandelier crashed down behind him.

Once again the swords clashed over the tables, but this time they had changed sides, and Gisburne was closer to the wall. Gisburne cut down and the swords locked, forming a cross in mid-air. With his left hand, he grabbed Robert's wrist, then pulled him over the table towards him. Robert somersaulted forward, the move bringing a fresh burst of pain from his wounded leg. At the same time, Gisburne reached out. An old serving-woman, clearing the tables, had been caught in the middle of the fight. Using her as a living shield, Gisburne pressed forward, bearing down on Robert. For a few vital seconds, Robert was powerless, unable to attack Gisburne for fear of harming the old woman. In those few seconds, Gisburne finished it. Suddenly leaping out from behind his shield, he twisted his blade round Robert's and jerked, sending Robert's sword flying.

Robert was forced back against the wall. His hands were empty.

The Sheriff, one hand clasped against his stomach, watched with eager eyes.

Gisburne drew Albion back for the final blow. There was nothing Robert could do.

But Gisburne didn't move. His face had changed – from triumph to incomprehension and again to fear. It was as if he were fighting with the air. The sword Albion was still held high above him, but he could not move it. And now the blade was beginning to shine, not reflecting the light, but shining with its own inner power. Gisburne groaned, his whole body shaking. Still he struggled to bring the blade down, to slice Robert's head from his neck. But he was helpless.

The blade was glowing now. Robert smelt something – the sickly smell of roasting flesh. Albion had become red-hot. It was burning the palm of Gisburne's hand.

Gisburne screamed.

The sword clattered to the ground. Gisburne sank to his knees, groaning, one hand cradled in the other.

Robert hesitated, then picked up the sword. It was cool to the touch. The glow had disappeared.

He ran out through a side door and into the main courtyard. Only one soldier tried to stop him as he seized a horse. It was the last thing the soldier ever did.

By the time the servants had come to the aid of the wounded Sheriff and the trembling steward, Robert of Huntingdon was gone.

It was a warm evening; the breeze was blowing softly through the forest, turning the cornfields into a gently rippling sea of burning gold. The autumn sun was setting behind Sherwood, shafts of light slanting through the leaves.

Robert stood with Albion in his hands, the point resting on the ground. The outlaws were with him ... Little John and Will Scarlet, Friar Tuck, Much, Nasir. And Marion. Marion was staying with them in Sherwood. After what had happened there could be no going back.

'Herne's son is my master,' she whispered. 'I cannot slay him.'

Robert looked down at the runes, engraved on the blade of Albion. Their mystery had at last been revealed to him. The sword itself had told him what, for so long, he had refused to acknowledge. He was Herne's son. The powers of light and darkness were his.

And there was Herne, in the form of a stag, silhouetted against the blood-red sky. The outlaws knelt before him and Robert knelt with them. Herne's voice called out.

'To help the weak, defend the helpless and fight against tyranny. So must it be – Robin i'the Hood.'

Robin i'the Hood.

Nobody would ever call him Robert of Huntingdon again. Even the Earl had disowned him. But he was not sad. That part of his life was over.

He was Robin Hood now. He always would be.

The hooded man.

ROBIN OF SHERWOOD

Richard Carpenter

A magical retelling of the legend of Robin Hood. Traditional adventure spiced with medieval mysticism and sorcery: the life and times of England's greatest hero.

England in the twelfth century is a land that has been firmly subjugated by the Normans. But scattered throughout the country there are still small areas of resistance, where bands of outlaws keep the flame of freedom alive . . .

ROBIN OF SHERWOOD AND THE HOUNDS OF LUCIFER

Richard Carpenter/Robin May

Robin Hood and his small, determined band battle on against the dangers that face the ordinary people of Sherwood: the brutal riders known as the Hounds of Lucifer, the machinations of the Sheriff of Nottingham, and, finally, the greatest enemy of all . . .

CATWEAZLE
Richard Carpenter

An incompetent eleventh-century magician arrives in the twentieth century and somehow muddles through. Very popular and hysterically funny.

THE SAGA OF ERIK THE VIKING
Terry Jones

A magnificent collection of stories about a valiant band of Vikings: potent, allusive, oddly familiar, yet completely original. A superb companion volume to FAIRY TALES, also illustrated by Michael Foreman.

THE APPRENTICES
Leon Garfield

A collection of the much-acclaimed Apprentices stories. Each one features a London trade and they are linked by recurring characters.

THE BRONZE BOW

Elizabeth George Speare

Daniel, a Jewish boy, is obsessed by hatred of the Roman invaders who crucified his father, until he hears a preacher named Jesus, and begins to wonder whether violence is the right answer. A Newbery Medal winner.

CHILDREN ON THE OREGON TRAIL

A. Rutgers van der Loeff

Stirring adventures of pioneering families heading westwards in their covered wagons.

CUE FOR TREASON

Geoffrey Trease

Peter Browning runs away from home and joins a band of strolling players. He becomes involved with Robert Cecil's secret service and a plot to kill Queen Elizabeth.

LEGIONS OF THE EAGLE

Henry Treece

Thirteen-year-old Gwydion had grown up during one of the few short periods of peace in the troubled history of early Britain. So he was both surprised and excited one day to see an old war-chariot being cleaned up, and blades being sharpened, in anticipation of a Roman attack. War was something Gwydion had not yet experienced. Little did he know what dangerous and astonishing adventures it was to lead him to.

THE GLORY GIRL

Betsy Byars

While the rest of her family enjoy the limelight as the Glory Gospel singers, Anna Glory has to content herself with selling the Glory record albums. She feels lonely and left out, because she cannot sing.

When their mysterious Uncle Newt is released from prison, it becomes clear that the Glorys are determined to have nothing to do with him – but Anna feels strangely drawn to this other family misfit . . .

SUMMER OF THE ZEPPELIN

Elsie McCutcheon

It's the First World War and while her father is fighting in France, Elvira lives with her stepmother Rhoda. But she runs away to an abandoned house, where she meets Bill, a German prisoner of war.

GOLDEN PENNIES
Graeme Farmer

A gripping adventure story set in Australia in 1851. Jack and Lucy go with their parents to Ballaret, where gold has just been discovered, and their story tells of the troubles that surround the whole family. Then things start to improve when Lucy finds three nuggets.

THE BOY WITH THE BRONZE AXE
Kathleen Fidler

An imaginative reconstruction of the way the Bronze Age probably spread to outlying Stone Age settlements.

UNDERGROUND TO CANADA
Barbara C. Smucker

Based on the true history of the Underground Railroad, this story tells of two negro slave girls who make the perilous journey north to freedom in Canada.

BONNIE DUNDEE
Rosemary Sutcliff

The exciting and romantic story of John Claverhouse, Viscount of Dundee, seen through the eyes of his devoted follower, Hugh Herriott.

This book belongs to...

Lynne Stewart
Abbey Arms Hotel
New Abbey
Dumfries
Scotland

DG2-8.B.U.